Clam
A Rainey Daye Cozy Mystery, book 1
by
Kathleen Suzette

Copyright © 2018 by Kathleen Suzette. All rights reserved. This book is a work of fiction. All names, characters, places and incidents are either products of the author's imagination, or used fictiously. Any resemblance to actual events, locales or persons, living or dead, is entirely coincidental. All rights reserved. No part of this book may be reproduced or transmitted in any form or by any means, electronically or mechanical, without permission in writing from the author or publisher.

Books by Kathleen Suzette:
Clam Chowder and a Murder
A Rainey Daye Cozy Mystery, book 1

Short Stack and a Murder
A Rainey Daye Cozy Mystery, book 2
Cherry Pie and a Murder
A Rainey Daye Cozy Mystery, book 3
Barbecue and a Murder
A Rainey Daye Cozy Mystery, book 4
Birthday Cake and a Murder
A Rainey Daye Cozy Mystery, book 5
Hot Cider and a Murder
A Rainey Daye Cozy Mystery, book 6
Roast Turkey and a Murder
A Rainey Daye Cozy Mystery, book 7

TABLE OF CONTENTS

Chapter One
Chapter two
Chapter three
Chapter Four
Chapter Five
Chapter six
Chapter Seven
Chapter Eight
Chapter Nine
Chapter Ten
Chapter Eleven
Chapter Twelve
Chapter Thirteen
Chapter Fourteen
Chapter Fifteen
Chapter Sixteen
Chapter Seventeen
Author Notes

Chapter One

"Rainey Jane Strong, I can't believe you're still alive. I would have thought that crazy mother of yours would have killed you by now."

I spun around, coming face to face with Celia Markson, the town busybody. Oh, the title wasn't official, but it may as well have been. She took her job seriously. I narrowed my eyes at her as I involuntarily cringed at how close she stood to me and then forced myself to smile.

"It's Rainey Daye. And I'm divorced," I corrected. Again. I had grown up in Sparrow, Idaho, but for some reason people had a hard time remembering I was divorced and going by my maiden name again. My married name had brought me a modest amount of fame and fortune and it seemed people didn't want me to part with it. I would have rather forgotten the fame, and even the fortune if I could have erased the last ten years of my life.

Celia rolled her eyes. "Just like your mother. She thinks she's right about everything, too," she said and burped, not bothering to cover her mouth or excuse herself. I took a step back as she reached into her coat pocket, searched for a moment, and then brought out her hand, still empty. "I've run out of peppermints. I need a peppermint, I've got indigestion." She held her hand out.

"Of course," I said, and fished in my apron pocket for one of the red and white striped peppermints we gave out to customers with their diner ticket. In my married life, I had been a blogger, cookbook writer, and did the weekly cooking segments on a morning show in New York. Post-divorce, I worked part-time at Sam's Diner. I was fine with it. Really, I was. I just didn't love the job like I had loved my previous career. Being at people's beck and call got on my nerves.

Celia popped the candy into her mouth and burped again. "Must have been something from breakfast. I've got to buy some antacids."

"Can I show you to a table?" I asked her, tucking my blond hair behind my ear and forcing myself to sound more chipper than I felt. If I wasn't nice she'd tell on me.

She waved me away like a bothersome fly and headed to an empty booth. Celia owned the Perfect Florist Shop on Main Street and was my mother's biggest competitor. My mother owned the Sparrow Flower Shop, and over the years, had been the subject of some of Celia's dirtiest rumors. Like when she told people my mother bought lead-contaminated vases from a foreign supplier. Or that my mother sold low-quality flowers that died twice as fast as the flowers she sold in her own shop. I was probably starring in a few of her rumors as we spoke, but they hadn't made their way back to me yet.

I picked up a menu from the hostess station and went to the booth Celia had chosen. A booth in my section.

"Would you like to look at a menu Celia, or do you know what you'd like?" I asked. Celia was in her early sixties and wore her blond hair cropped short with wide brown streaks going through it. She was just over five feet tall and she wore too much blue eye shadow; trying to relive her youth, I thought. Her wrists were covered in gold bracelets and clinked when she waved her hands around. She liked attention.

"I want some iced tea," she said, ignoring the menu I held out to her. "And clam chowder. You know I only order clam chowder. There's nothing else worth eating here. The burgers are greasy and the fries are limp. Don't get me started on the chili."

I pulled my order book and a pen out of my apron pocket and jotted down her order. Celia was a real breath of fresh air. "Got it. I'll be right back with your iced tea."

"And I don't want any of those saltines. You tell Sam I said they get stale. I want the oyster crackers," she said, peering out the window beside her booth. She coughed without covering her mouth, her gaze never leaving the window.

"I certainly will," I said and headed to the kitchen. It was just after noon and the diner was hopping. Sam's was only open for breakfast and lunch and we sold the best clam chowder in the state of Idaho.

"Celia Markson's out there and she wants oyster crackers, not saltines," I said to Sam as he flipped hamburger patties on the grill. I chuckled. "We don't have oyster crackers and she's going to have a fit." I put the ticket on the metal order holder and watched him flip burgers.

"Yeah we do," Sam said, as he dodged the flames that flared when the fat from the patties dripped down onto the fire.

"Since when?" I asked as Luanne, one of the other waitresses, brushed past me to hang an order next to the one I had just put up.

"Since my last shopping trip," Sam said. "We've got to keep the customers happy, right?" He looked at me with a sly grin.

I rolled my eyes at him. Sam was a good boss, low-key and low drama, but I hated that he caved to that busybody. She was a pest, and I didn't care for her any more than my mother did.

I headed over to the soft drink station and filled a red striped plastic glass with ice. We weren't fancy at Sam's, but the food more than made up for it. And not just the clam chowder, either. Everything on the menu was mouth-watering, in spite of what Celia said. When tourists came to Sparrow to spend time at the Salmon River, most made it a point to eat at Sam's.

Luanne joined me at the soft drink station. "I see you got Celia Markson," she said with a smirk.

I rolled my eyes. "Lucky me," I said, and filled the glass with tea. I picked up a slice of lemon and hung it on the edge of the glass. Glancing up, I saw a line forming at the hostess station and I sighed. I reminded myself to reconsider my decision to take a job at the diner. It didn't pay much, but I had to admit that the tips were good. Then I reminded myself I could work here until I found something I really wanted to do.

"Don't let her get to you. She'll only be in here, what? Forty-five minutes? An hour, tops," Luanne said helpfully. It was easy for her to be optimistic about Celia when she wasn't eating in her section.

"And she'll run me ragged every minute. It's way too busy in here today to put up with her," I said. I picked up the glass of tea and headed to Celia's table.

"Yup," she said. "She will."

"Here you go, Celia," I said brightly, setting the glass of tea in front of her.

"Oh no, you take that back, Rainey Strong," Celia said, wrinkling up her nose and pointing to the glass as if I had offered her poison.

"What? Why?" I asked, without correcting her about my last name again.

"How many years have I been coming to this diner?" she asked, pursing her lips together.

I shrugged. "I don't know. I've only been working here for six months."

"Twenty years. And everyone knows I do not take lemon with my tea. I've told you that before. You go back there and make me a fresh glass of tea without the lemon. And don't think you can disappear around the corner and take the lemon slice off the rim and bring back the same glass. I'll know if you try that."

I gritted my teeth against the words that wanted to come out of my mouth and forced the muscles in my face to smile. "Why certainly, Celia. I'd love to do that for you." *I have nothing better to do with my time.*

"I thought you would," she said with a nod.

I spun around and nearly ran into Diane, the other waitress on duty. "Oh, sorry Diane," I said, as I held the glass steady.

"Wow," Diane said. "It's a madhouse in here today."

"Sure is," I said and hurried back to the drink station. I was sorely tempted to take the lemon slice off the glass and take it back to Celia but I figured that was taking my life into my hands. "Sam, how's that clam chowder coming?"

He bent to look through the pass-through window and eyed me. "There's a big pot ready to go. Can you take care of it for me? I've got my hands full."

I sighed. I had other tables waiting for me to take their orders. "Yeah, I got it." I filled a fresh glass with ice and tea and left the glass at the soft drink station while I got the soup. The clam chowder was gently simmering on the front stove burner and I ladled some into a bowl and grabbed a basket of wrapped saltines.

"Oyster crackers," Sam reminded me.

"Fine," I murmured and put the basket down. There was one basket with small packages of oyster crackers, so I grabbed two of the packages, put them in my apron pocket, and headed to pick up the tea on my way back to Celia's table.

"Here we are," I said and set the glass and bowl in front of her. "It's hot, so be careful." I grabbed the packages of oyster crackers from my apron pocket and laid them on the table in front of her.

"I need another peppermint," she said without commenting on the clam chowder or tea.

"Sure," I said and fished out two peppermints.

She burped and snatched the peppermints from my hand. Her face was pasty white, and she looked tired. Mascara was smeared beneath her eyes and something seemed off about her, but I couldn't put my finger on what it was.

"Well, enjoy your meal," I said and forced myself to smile again.

Her lips were on the glass of tea and she pulled it away, grimacing.

"What did I tell you about just removing the slice of lemon? I told you I would know it!" she screeched.

"What? That's a fresh glass," I said as the smile left my lips. "I just poured it."

She glared at me. "Do you really think I'm that stupid? Do you?"

I shook my head. "No ma'am. But I got a fresh glass from the cupboard, I promise."

She rolled her eyes. "Rainey Jane Strong. I can taste the lemon. You get Sam out here right now. I will not tolerate this disrespect! No wonder your husband left you!"

The floor dropped out from under my feet and I glanced around at the other diners staring in our direction. Heat flamed up in my cheeks and I wished I had a hole to crawl into. I wanted to tell her I left Craig because he was a cheater, but it was none of her business. I could feel all eyes on me. Celia was loud even when she wasn't trying to be and since she never passed up a chance to be the center of attention, she was very loud now.

"Celia, you can see by all the customers here that Sam is very busy in the kitchen. I'll just get you another fresh glass." I reached for the glass in front of her and she reached out and grabbed hold of my wrist.

"I want to talk to Sam. Now," she said through gritted teeth.

My eyes met hers and I could see they were bloodshot. Even for Celia, this behavior seemed a little off. Had she been drinking? I couldn't remember ever seeing her drink before.

"Sure, Celia," I said evenly. "I'll get Sam. But you might have to wait a bit. In the meantime, I'll get you some fresh tea."

Her grip tightened on my wrist for a moment, and then she released it without looking at me. I forced myself to smile and left without the glass of tea. I wasn't sure what was up with Celia, but I didn't need the attention. My marriage was my business, and she needed to keep her nose out of it. I hurried to the kitchen to talk to Sam.

"Celia is demanding to see you at her table," I said to Sam when I got to the kitchen. "I told her you were busy and it might be a bit. Maybe she'll get tired of waiting and leave."

"Oh?" Sam asked, turning toward me with a silver spatula in his hand. "What's going on?"

"She sent me back with her glass of iced tea because I put lemon on the rim of the glass. She wanted another one, and she warned me not to just remove the lemon from the glass and bring it back. So, I got a fresh glass, and she claims it's the original glass. She says she can tell a lemon has been on the rim, but I swear I brought her a fresh glass."

"She doesn't like lemon," he said. He laid the spatula down. "Watch these burgers, will you?"

"What? Sam, you've got more important things to do than placate that woman," I insisted. Sam didn't answer me on his way out of the kitchen.

I sighed and went to the grill. The kitchen was hot and humid. A long tendril of my hair had escaped the bun at the back of my head and I pushed it back into my plastic hairclip and then flipped a hamburger patty. That woman had always been trouble. I didn't know why Sam bothered with her.

Chapter two

CLAM CHOWDER AND A MURDER

I tried not to be irritated, but I was. Celia was a pain and there wasn't a nicer way to put it. While the orders stacked up, Sam stood at Celia's table trying to appease her. I rolled my eyes at Diane when she passed.

"Gotta love that man. He aims to please," she said with a chuckle.

"You can't please everyone though," I pointed out, sulking. I was too old to behave that way, but that woman got on my nerves.

Luanne had taken over the grill and slid my order for table nine across the counter to me. "Order up."

"This is the wrong time for Sam to leave the grill," I grumbled and picked up my order. "I don't know what he's thinking. We're too busy to waste time on someone like Celia Markson."

"Everything cool in here?" Sam said, six inches from my ear.

I jumped and shot Luanne a look. She could have given me a warning that he was right behind me. "Everything's great," I said. The man needed bells on his shoes.

As I passed Celia's table, she was blowing on a spoonful of hot chowder. Her boyfriend, Gerald Vance, was standing at the side of her table and I wondered if they would flag me down and order something for him. While they were deep in conversation, I slipped past them and attended to table nine.

The rest of the lunch shift was bustling, but by two o'clock the diner was almost empty. Remembering Celia, I glanced over at her table. I hadn't completely forgotten her, but I had put off checking up on her. Gerald had never ordered anything and the table was now empty. I sighed and wondered if she had stiffed us on the bill. Probably not. Too many people had seen her make a scene earlier and since she was a business owner, she couldn't afford to stiff another business.

I went to her table and picked up her half-eaten bowl of soup. It was an odd sight. Almost no one left Sam's clam chowder behind. They either finished it or took a to-go container with them.

"My feet hurt," Diane groaned.

"You've been here all day. Why don't you go home and I'll finish cleaning up?" I offered.

"This place is a mess. I couldn't do that to you," she said, running a white dishcloth over table four. Georgia Johnson was supposed to relieve Diane for the lunch shift, but she had called in sick and Diane got stuck working both shifts. I knew her feet had to be killing her.

"It's fine," I assured her. "We'll be locking the door pretty soon, anyway."

That was an advantage to working in a place that only served breakfast and lunch. We locked up as soon as the place cleared out. After we cleaned up, we went home to enjoy the rest of the afternoon.

"Well, you don't have to argue with me about it then," she said and laid her dishcloth on the cleaning cart.

I liked Diane. She was in her late forties with short blond hair and blue eyes. She could work circles around most people and I never had to worry that she wouldn't be on her game. She had been a waitress since high school.

"I'll see you," I said as she passed me to say goodnight to Sam and Luanne.

"See you," she said. "Thanks again."

I kept one eye on the front door and the other on the dirty tables. If no one stopped in, we would close by two-thirty and be home as soon as we could get things cleaned up. If stragglers stopped in though, we would stay as long as we had to.

A few minutes later, after our last customer had left, Sam walked over to the door and locked it. The clock said 2:13.

"Closing early?" I asked as I wiped down the last table.

He shrugged. "I'm out of hamburger patties and the clam chowder's all gone. I don't see what it will hurt. Besides, I'm tight with the boss," he said with a wink.

I chuckled. "Thank goodness for that." Sam had a sweet, boyish charm about him. He was slightly built and had dimples that made him attractive in a boy-next-door kind of way and besides that, he was an all-around nice guy.

Luanne came out of the supply closet with the vacuum and got to work on the dining room floor. It was a mess after the busy day.

I began filling the salt and pepper shakers and the ketchup bottles. I had never thought I would be a waitress. Being a mini-celebrity had been fun while it lasted, but when I divorced my big-time publisher husband, I found out that all the people I thought were my friends were actually his. They disappeared, and I lost my job on the morning show for dubious reasons. When negative blog reviews for my cookbooks appeared all over the Internet and I got hateful comments on my own blog, I decided I needed a change. And here I was, back in the small Idaho town I had grown up in. Sparrow, Idaho, population: about 20,000. Sparrow had a real hometown atmosphere, and it felt good to be home. The divorce was a necessity, and I was determined to pick myself up and get on with my life. I didn't yet know exactly what it was I was going to do with my life, but I would figure it out. Eventually.

The three of us tidied up as fast as we could manage while our dishwasher, Ron White, worked on the kitchen. I was learning a lot about efficiency working here at the diner, and after six months, I was really just beginning to feel competent.

We finished up and walked out the door together. My car was parked at the far end of the parking lot, so I said my goodbyes and walked my aching feet to my car. Being on my feet for hours at a time was something I never enjoyed, but it was part of the job, so I bought cushy insoles and sucked it up.

There was an older gold-colored Buick parked two spaces over from my car. I sighed. People were forever parking in our lot and getting out to walk the strip of touristy shops down the middle of town. I didn't blame them. Sparrow was a quaint mountain town with candy, gift, and antique shops that dotted Main Street. The Snake River and great camping locations drew hunters and campers from several states around and Sparrow did its best to provide supplies and other diversions should people get tired of the great outdoors.

I unlocked my car and glanced over at the Buick. There was someone slumped over the steering wheel. Were they looking for something on the floor? I got into my car and turned to look again. After watching the person in the Buick for a minute or so, I realized they didn't seem to be moving. That was strange. I got out of my car and went around to the driver's side of the Buick, keeping an eye on whoever was behind the wheel.

My foot crunched on something and I stopped. I looked down and moved my foot. It was a crushed peppermint like the kind we gave out to all the customers. I kicked it aside and looked at the car again. The person inside still wasn't moving, so I knocked on the window. When they didn't stir, my heart started to beat faster. Were they sick? I swallowed.

I knocked again, and when there was still no response, I put my hand on the door handle and carefully opened the door. The hint of perfume inside the car and the leopard print scarf she was wearing told me it was a woman.

"Ma'am?" I asked. I reached a hand out to shake her. "Are you okay? Ma'am?" I looked over my shoulder at Sam and Luanne getting into their cars.

"Excuse me? Ma'am?" I said loudly to the woman.

My heart pounded when she still didn't respond, so I gently leaned the woman back in the seat. That was when I screamed.

Celia.

Chapter three

I had never seen a dead person before. I was thirty-five-years-old, and I had been to three funerals in my life. They had all been closed casket. Never mind having touched a dead person because I hadn't done that either.

"I can't believe it," Sam said for what must have been the fifteenth time. When I realized Celia was dead, I had screamed and frantically waved at Sam and Luanne. We were now leaning against Luanne's car, a safe distance from the EMTs that had looked Celia over and then covered up her body. The police had arrived and were taking pictures and performing an investigation. We were told to stay put for the time being.

"I can't believe it, either," I said. And I couldn't. Celia may have been a thorn in my side, but I had never wished her dead. I might have wished she had lost the ability to speak, but I did not wish her dead.

"She probably had a heart attack," Luanne said. "Eating all that clam chowder isn't good for you."

I looked at her. "Seriously, Luanne?" Luanne had a tendency to say whatever popped into her mind.

She nodded, twirling a lock of her brown hair. "That's all she ever ordered. It was probably a heart attack caused by Sam's clam chowder. All that butter and heavy cream takes a toll on your heart."

"Do you think so?" Sam asked, looking at me. His forehead was creased with worry lines and his eyes were turning red.

I sighed and shook my head. Luanne was clueless. "I seriously don't think so. And even if it was, you didn't force it down her throat."

"Unless there was blood," Luanne said, looking at me. "Was there blood? Because if there was, then I don't think it was a heart attack."

I rolled my eyes and groaned. "Seriously, Luanne?" I repeated.

"Was there blood?" she asked again.

I shook my head, and I felt myself get light-headed. Everything was a blur, but I was pretty sure I hadn't seen blood. What I did see was Celia staring at me wide-eyed and slack-jawed, a whitish substance had run out her mouth and down her chin. I never wanted to see anything like that again.

"I'd rather not talk about the details," Sam said, folding his arms across his chest and looking down at his feet.

"I'm with you on that," I murmured. I needed a way to scrub the image of Celia's face from my mind.

As we talked, an unmarked black sedan pulled up and parked near the ambulance. A tall, dark-haired man in a suit got out and headed over to one of the police officers. After a minute, the officer pointed toward us and the man in the suit looked in our direction.

"He's coming over," Luanne said. "Do either of you know who he is? I like tall and handsome."

"Nope," I said. In a small town you know almost everyone, or have at least seen them around town, and he didn't look familiar.

Sam shook his head but didn't say anything. His arms were still crossed over his chest and he looked like a man with a lot on his mind.

CLAM CHOWDER AND A MURDER 21

The stranger in the suit looked very business-like as he strode toward us, his long legs quickly covering the distance between us. He stopped two feet in front of us and nodded.

I was drawn to his bright green eyes, and in another setting, I would have smiled and made conversation. Whoever he was, he was handsome.

"Hello," he said. "My name is Detective Cade Starkey. I'm with the Sparrow police department. The officer told me you all found the victim and I'd like to ask some questions."

"Celia," I said.

He looked at me, questioning. His chocolate brown hair shone in the afternoon sun and I wondered what kind of product he used to make it shine like that.

"Celia?" he asked me.

I cleared my throat. I didn't like Celia, but it bothered me to hear her referred to as 'the victim'. "Her name is Celia Markson," I repeated. "Was, I mean. Her name was Celia Markson."

He nodded and without comment took a notebook and pen out of his coat pocket.

"I'll need your names," he said, pen poised over his notepad.

"Rainey Daye," I said and watched as his eyebrows went up and he hesitated before writing my name in his book.

"Rainey Daye?" he asked.

I nodded. "Rainey Daye," I repeated, trying not to sound defensive.

"I'm Sam Stevens and I own the diner," Sam said.

"I'm Luanne Merrill," Luanne said in a sexy voice. I shot her a look, but she ignored me as she looked the detective up and down.

"Were you all together when the body was discovered?" he asked.

I shook my head. "I saw Celia's body when I went to my car to go home. I mean, I didn't know it was her body. I didn't know who it was when I first saw her. I just saw someone slumped over the steering wheel, so I checked on her. I called the others over when I realized it was Celia and she was dead."

"She screamed. She screamed really loud, and we drove across the parking lot to see what was up," Luanne added, nodding her head.

I shot her another look.

"And did you check for a pulse immediately?" he asked me, ignoring Luanne.

I stared at him, and then slowly shook my head. "I guess I didn't think about it."

"She was clearly dead," Sam said dryly. "I checked to see if she was breathing. Her body was cold."

The detective nodded and made another note. "I take it you all knew her?"

"She was a customer," I supplied. The fact that she was my mother's one and only business rival was at the back of my mind, but I kept it to myself.

"She came to the diner frequently," Sam said, unfolding his arms and shoving his hands into his pockets.

"And did you know her?" he asked Luanne.

"Yes, I knew her. She owned the Perfect Florist Shop on Main Street. I bought flowers from her twice. She had the freshest flowers in town."

I looked at Luanne and tried not to scowl, but Luanne was an airhead and she would talk forever if someone didn't stop her.

"She did indeed own a florist shop in town," I supplied. "She came in today and ordered clam chowder. She always ordered clam chowder."

"What is your job at the diner?" he asked me without looking up.

"I'm a waitress. Luanne and I are both waitresses. We were getting off work and going home when I found her." I was starting to repeat myself and I hoped he didn't notice. I wasn't guilty of anything, but for some reason, I felt guilty.

"Did you wait on her?" he asked, looking up now.

I couldn't read this Cade Starkey. I was sure he must not be from around here since I hadn't seen him before, and he wasn't very friendly.

"I did," I said. "She ordered iced tea and clam chowder." I was repeating myself again. My cheeks flushed, and I told myself to stop.

"Rainey had an argument with Celia," Luanne informed him.

I looked at Luanne wide-eyed. *What was she thinking?*

The detective looked up at me again and seemed to study me a moment. "What did you argue about?"

I opened my mouth and then closed it. My heart was pounding in my chest and my tongue suddenly felt like sandpaper. "Iced tea. She thought I had put a slice of lemon on the rim of the glass of iced tea, but I didn't. I mean, I did on the first glass, but not on the replacement. And it wasn't an argument, really. She thought I had made a mistake, and I told her I hadn't. That's all." I shrugged to show him it was a mistake, and I was innocent.

He narrowed his eyes at me. "You argued about iced tea and lemon?"

"No!" I said too quickly. "I mean, no. Like I said, we didn't argue. She was kind of a fussy customer and she wasn't happy about the lemon. I went back and got her a fresh glass of tea without lemon." I looked at Sam for help, but he remained tight-lipped.

"That's got to be frustrating," he said, sounding bored. "Did anything seem out of the ordinary?"

I shook my head. "No, nothing. And I don't mind difficult customers. I get paid to serve them just like everybody else," I said and smiled. Maybe a smile would convince him I was telling the truth. "Oh, wait. She had heartburn and asked for a peppermint."

His eyebrows furrowed. "A peppermint?"

"Yes, we give them out to the customers when they pay their bills," I said and fished one out of my pocket to show him. "My mother says peppermint helps your stomach." As soon as I said it, I felt like an idiot. Did he really care what my mother said about peppermints?

He nodded slowly, and I was sure he also thought I was an idiot.

"Is there anything anyone else would like to add?" he asked, looking at Sam and Luanne.

"Do you think she had a heart attack?" I asked, spitting the words out quickly.

He shrugged and gave me a tight-lipped smile. "It's really too early to know anything. We'll have to wait for the coroner to release her body and then there will probably be an autopsy. Do you know if Ms. Markson had heart problems?"

My mouth dropped open. I closed it and shook my head. "I don't know. She never mentioned it." Now I really was an idiot. I was making a diagnosis of a dead woman, based on what? The fact that she was dead?

He narrowed his eyes at me again. "I'll need contact information for all three of you in case we have questions."

As he took our info, I kicked myself mentally. I should have let Luanne keep talking and let her look like a fool instead of volunteering for that position.

"Great. I'm sure I'll be in touch. You're free to go," he said and headed back to the other officers without looking back.

I turned to Luanne. "Why did you tell him I argued with Celia?" I hissed.

"Because you did," she said, nodding that empty head of hers.

"I did not!" I hissed again.

"Why don't we all go home and get some rest?" Sam suggested wearily. "It's been a long day."

"Fine. I'll see you two tomorrow," I said and headed to my car.

When I got into my car, I looked over at Cade Starkey. He was just a detective doing his job. But why did I feel nervous about him asking perfectly normal questions? I shook myself. My mind was running away with me and I needed to go home.

Chapter Four

"I have terrible news," I announced when I walked through the door of my mother's house. I had been living there since I moved back to town. My plans had been to move to an apartment as soon as possible, but somehow one week had turned into a month and then to six months.

Mom looked up from the pot roast she was sprinkling with black pepper.

"What terrible news?" Stormy asked from her place beside Mom. Stormy was my identical twin sister. Yeah, my mother named her twins Rainey and Stormy and with a last name like Daye, the jokes from people that think they're clever never stop. Go figure.

Stormy was married and had five kids and frequently stopped by to visit. I suspected she needed a break from the kids.

"What's going on?" Mom asked. A red curl fell across her forehead and she pushed it back.

"Celia Markson is dead."

Mom frowned, thought about it a moment, and then smiled. "And this is terrible, why?"

People say I get my personality from my mother, but I swear she's more of a smart aleck than I have ever been.

"Mom, I'm serious," I said, crossing the living room to the kitchen pass-through. "She died in the diner parking lot."

"Celia's dead? What happened?" Stormy asked with the appropriate level of interest.

I shook my head. "I don't know. I hope it was a heart attack or an aneurysm or some other natural cause, but she looked really bad when I found her."

Mom gasped. "You found her? Where was she?"

I nodded, thankful she was finally showing the appropriate level of concern. "She was in her car and her car was parked near my car in the diner parking lot. I saw her slumped over the steering wheel and I checked on her. I didn't see any blood or anything suspicious, but her mouth and eyes were wide open."

Mom made a face. "I'm sorry, honey. That must have been terrible to find her that way."

"It was. I can't believe it. It was awful," I said with a whine in my voice. "A detective showed up and was asking questions and Luanne told him Celia and I had an argument. Can you believe she said that?"

"Did you argue with Celia?" Stormy asked, taking a sip from her water bottle. Stormy was currently wearing her blond hair almost exactly like mine. Long and straight. She was a copycat like that.

"You know Celia. Her iced tea wasn't perfect, and she made a stink about it. It wasn't an actual argument, but Luanne told the detective it was." I looked from Stormy to my mother. "I don't know if he believed her or not."

"I'm sure it will be fine," Stormy said, coming around to where I stood and giving my shoulders a squeeze. "She probably had a heart attack. Besides, having an argument with someone doesn't mean you killed them."

"But that detective looked like a dog after a bone. I really think he's suspicious of me." I might have been embellishing a bit, but my imagination had run wild on the drive home.

"Rainey, they have to have more evidence than just the fact that you had an argument with her. I'm sure it will be death by natural causes anyway," Stormy assured me.

I nodded, thankful she was here to quiet my fears. The years I had spent in New York without her had made me feel like I had a hole in my heart. I missed my twin.

After high school, I went to college and Stormy stayed in Sparrow, married her high school sweetheart, and started popping out kids. She was my best friend, and I wanted to believe she was right about everything being okay, but I was still worried.

"I'm sure Celia Markson had plenty of people that would have wanted her dead. Including me. But of course, I didn't argue with her in public and I didn't kill her," Mom said, grinding more pepper onto the roast.

"Thanks for the support, Mom. And if I were you, I wouldn't go around saying you wanted her dead. At least, not until they rule her death as natural causes," I said and went to the refrigerator for a bottle of water. Mom had renovated an old Victorian house and furnished it with both vintage and antique pieces. The refrigerator was a 1940 General Electric. She had it painted a creamy yellow to match a restored yellow 1940 O'Keefe and Merritt Town and Country stove. The refrigerator was cute and had been refurbished, but it was small. There was a newer side-by-side fridge in the garage to hold the excess groceries.

"Rainey, you're letting your imagination run away with you. You always do that. I'm sure she had a heart attack," Mom said, chopping an onion.

"Yes, look on the bright side. She probably died from poor health," Stormy said with a giggle.

I twisted the top off my bottle of water. I hoped they were right, but Celia was a jogger. I frequently saw her running the neighborhood in the early mornings. She may have been in her early sixties, but she didn't look or act it.

"How are the kids?" I asked Stormy, changing the subject.

She sighed. "Natalie is insisting she's fine with moving to California to go to college. But she's always been so shy. I don't know how she'll survive that far from home." Tears sprang to her eyes, and she blinked them back.

"Maybe some independence will be good for her," I said. "I bet she'll really bloom once she's out on her own." Stormy had a case of empty nest syndrome, except that with four other children, the nest wasn't really going to be empty.

"I know. That's what Bob says. She'll be fine," she said sounding unconvinced. She took another sip from the bottle of water she held in her hands.

"One good thing about Celia's death," Mom said, putting the casserole dish with roast into the oven. "I won't have customers coming into the shop and telling me how Celia's gossiping about me."

"A silver lining," I said, nodding and trying to look serious.

Stormy giggled. "You two are too much. Mom, I'm sure you feel at least a little sorry that she's gone."

"Nope, can't say that I do," Mom said, going to the sink to wash her hands. The deep farmer's sink was filled with dirty dishes and she opened the dishwasher door. The dishwasher wasn't vintage or antique, but it was a necessity.

"Mom, don't say that," I said, leaning against the white farmhouse table.

"Why not, Rainey?"

"Because it's just wrong. You always said not to talk ill of the dead," I reminded her. "And why aren't you at the flower shop right now? It's still open."

"I decided to come home early and put a nice roast in the oven so my darling daughter would have a hot meal for dinner. Besides, Donna's taking care of things. She's been with me for almost a year now and is perfectly capable of handling it. And you're right. I shouldn't speak ill of the dead. I'm sorry." She turned and gave me a wicked grin.

"You're incorrigible," I said, shaking my head.

"I've got to get home and make dinner. Bob's probably already home," Stormy said. "I've only got a few more months of family dinners with Natalie, after all."

"Stormy, that was the whole point of your job. You raised your kids to grow up and live amazing lives," I pointed out. "You're a wonderful mother and Natalie is a smart, sensible girl. She'll be fine."

"And if you're lucky, they'll come back and live with you forever," Mom said without turning around.

"Not forever, Mom. Not forever," I said, and walked Stormy to the door.

"Don't worry about Celia's death," Stormy said on the doorstep. "I'm sure she died of natural causes."

"I know, you're right," I said with a nod. I knew my imagination was running away with me and I needed to settle down.

"See you later," she said and headed to her car.

I sighed and watched her go. Celia's face with her blank staring eyes flashed across my mind and I shivered.

It's going to be fine.

Chapter Five

It was three days after I'd discovered Celia Markson's body and I was late for work. I'd forgotten to set the alarm on my phone and I was dreaming of sleeping, all nice and snug in my bed. I was enjoying the dream immensely when suddenly the floor dropped out from under my bed and it was suspended above the clouds. All would have been rosy, except that whatever was holding the bed in the air suddenly dropped it and I was hurtling toward the earth. When I jumped in my sleep, it woke me and I realized I was late to work.

I dressed at lightning speed with my heart pounding in my chest. It was a waste of adrenaline though. Sam wouldn't have blinked at my tardiness. He was too laid back to berate me for not making it in on time, but I was the kind of person that was reliable to a fault and being late went against everything I believed in.

I was in such a hurry that I missed the black unmarked police car sitting near the front of the diner.

"Hi, Rainey," Keith Sparks, a local handyman said as he held the door open for me to speed through.

"Hey, Keith," I said without slowing down.

"Late?" he asked with a chuckle.

It wasn't funny. I was rarely ever late. I couldn't stand when anyone showed up late. It gave me anxiety.

"Sorry I'm late, Sam," I said and skidded to a stop when I saw Detective Cade Starkey standing near the cash register.

I stared at him wide-eyed. I don't know why, but I did. There was something about that man that made me nervous. It may have been the gun beneath his coat or the handcuffs I was sure

CLAM CHOWDER AND A MURDER

he had concealed somewhere on his person, but the guy gave me the heebie-jeebies.

"Ms. Daye," he greeted me, sounding bored. I wondered if he was ever anything but bored.

"Hi," I said breathing hard, and then I looked at Sam, hoping he would rescue me from having to talk to the detective.

Sam shrugged. "Hi, Rainey."

"Sorry, I'm a little late," I said, glancing at the clock behind the counter. My heart skipped a beat. I was nearly twenty minutes late. "I'll get an apron."

Sam cleared his throat and his eyes went to the detective. "Detective Starkey would like to have a word with you."

"What?" I said, looking at the detective and then back to Sam. "Why? Why does he want to have a word with me?"

"I just have a few questions," the detective said, taking a step toward me.

I looked at Sam again. "But I'm already late for work. I've got to get on the floor and take orders."

"He said it would only take a minute," Sam said apologetically.

I looked back at the detective and nodded. "Um, sure." My heart was pounding in my ears and I told myself to calm down. If I behaved as if I had something to feel guilty about, the detective was bound to think I *was* guilty of something.

"You can use the break room, Detective," Sam said to him, and then he turned around and headed back to the kitchen.

I looked over at the detective again and forced myself to smile. "Come on back." *It will be fine.*

I turned toward the hallway that led to the back and Carlisle Garlock caught my eye, giving me a nod. Carlisle was a morning regular and was a nice guy. I nodded back and hoped he would say a little prayer for me.

The detective followed me back past the kitchen and into a small room we used for storage. There was a round wooden table with three chairs back there. Sam called it the break room, but no one ever took a break back there. The top of the table was nearly covered in canned goods.

"Um, why don't you have a seat?" I said, heading toward the chair with the least amount of items on it. I picked up the packages of napkins, straws, and a box of powdered milk from the chair, moving them to the far end of the table. Next, I began picking up the canned goods from the table directly in front of the chair I had offered him.

"It's okay, you don't have to move everything," the detective said. "I'll only take a minute of your time. I'm sure the diner will be crowded for breakfast soon and I don't want to keep you long."

I inhaled and kept gathering up the canned goods, happy he wouldn't be here long. "It will only take a moment," I said and carried the cans to the far end of the table, depositing them next to the napkins and straws. "There. That's a little better." I turned to the chair farthest away from the one I had cleared for him and began clearing it for myself.

He sat down in his freshly cleared chair and I sat in mine, folding my hands in my lap like a kindergartener waiting for story time. The stacked up cans on the table nearly obstructed my view of him, so I leaned to the side a little and looked at him, unsure of what I should do next. I smiled. Smiling was my go-to fix-all.

"Can you tell me in detail what happened the other day with Celia Markson?" he asked me, pulling a notebook out of his jacket pocket.

"Um—well, like I said before, she came in, asked for a peppermint and gave me her order. I brought her some clam chowder and iced tea with lemon. She didn't like lemon in her tea, so I brought her a fresh glass." I shrugged, trying to look innocent, but not sure I managed it.

He made a note before looking up at me. "Was there anything unusual about her? Did she mention anything out of the ordinary?"

I shook my head. "Not at all. Why?"

He studied me for what felt like a moment longer than was necessary before answering. "The medical examiner has conducted an autopsy and while the toxicology report isn't back yet, he feels Ms. Markson was poisoned."

I gasped. "Poisoned? How terrible! Wait. You're asking me these questions because she was poisoned?"

He gave me a curt nod. "It's just part of the investigation, Ms. Daye. You mentioned a peppermint? You said something the other day about that. Do you think that's significant for some reason?"

"That's right," I said, capitalizing on this fact. "She said she had heartburn and her breakfast wasn't sitting well with her. Maybe it was poison that wasn't sitting well with her?" The idea had just occurred to me. If she had heartburn, that was really poisoning that occurred before she came into the diner, then there was no way I could be accused of killing her. As long as he would believe Celia had come into the diner already poisoned, anyway.

He narrowed his eyes at me. "Only time will tell if that was the case."

I tried not to take in the fact that the detective was attractive. He was the enemy. Or rather, he was the enemy if he was looking in my direction regarding Celia's death.

I nodded. "Poor Celia. It must have been awful. Dying from poisoning, I mean."

"Someone brought up the fact that you argued with Ms. Markson. Not just the day she died, but on other occasions as well. Did you have ongoing issues with her?"

I gasped again. "What? Who told you that? I did not have ongoing issues with her!"

He looked me in the eye for a moment and then made another note. "Did she eat here often?"

"I guess it was often. Maybe once a week. Sometimes more, sometimes less. But I did not argue with her regularly," I explained. I needed him to believe that. "Can you make a note of that? She was a difficult person and no one here liked to see her come in. In fact, if you check around town, you'll find that she wasn't well liked, but I was always polite to her."

"Really? And why would people not like her?"

I shrugged. "She talked about people all the time. She liked to stir up trouble." I glanced at the clock on the wall. He had already been here longer than the minute he had promised and I hoped he would leave soon.

"Is there anything else you'd like to say about what happened?"

I shook my head. "No, not really. I feel very bad that Celia died like she did. It's terrible."

"Tell me, does your mother own a flower shop in town?" he asked, looking directly into my eyes again.

I opened my mouth and then closed it like a fish suddenly pulled out of the water. "She does," I said after a moment. "What does that have to do with anything?"

He shrugged. "It's just something that came up in my investigation. Someone mentioned it."

My heart began pounding in my chest again. "Now, you just hold on. Just because my mother owns a competing business doesn't mean anything. Is that what you're saying? Because it sounds like that's what you're saying." My head nodded like a bobble-head doll.

He held up one hand to me. "Hold on. I'm new to town and I don't know anyone or anything about this place. Someone mentioned it, and I was curious."

I nodded again and that bobble-head doll feeling came back to me. Ever since I got called into the principal's office in the second grade for a crime I didn't commit, I had had issues with authority figures. But I did not steal Missy Gain's milk money then, and I did not poison Celia Markson now. I told myself to calm down. "Yes, well, my mother does own the other flower shop in town. There was a third one, but the owner, Max Bevins, retired last year. I don't know why he didn't sell the shop when he retired, but he didn't. Several years ago, there was a fourth flower shop, but it burned down."

"So your mother stood to gain a lot by being the only florist in town?" he asked, looking at me steadily.

"Now, wait a minute. I don't like where this is going," I began and silently cursed Max Bevins for not selling his shop when he retired. At the time my mother had been thrilled there would be one less competitor, but now I wished he had sold the business. "I think you're off base here. My mother would never kill anyone."

"I'm kidding," he said with a hint of a smile on his lips. "You do get excited easily, don't you?"

I huffed air out of my mouth. "No, I do not get excited easily and I don't see anything funny here," I said, feeling anger rising up on the inside. When I lived in New York, I had taken up kickboxing for self-defense and if this guy hadn't had a gun, I might have given him a kick to his shins he wouldn't soon forget.

"You have a quick temper, don't you Ms. Daye?"

I narrowed my eyes at him. "I do not have a quick temper," I said as evenly as I could manage. "I'm just a little flustered because I was late to work. I hate being late."

He smiled again, but it wasn't a friendly smile. It was more a smile of satisfaction; as if he had gotten what he came for. "I appreciate your cooperation," he said, getting to his feet and ignoring my comment. "I'll be in touch if I have any other questions."

"I'm sure you will," I said standing up. "I bet there are a lot of other people to interview."

"I've interviewed everyone here at the diner. You were the last. Thanks again for your help." With that, he turned and walked out of the room.

I took a deep breath and watched him go. There was nothing to worry about, right? If I hadn't been flustered from being late to work, I would have been calmer, but as it was, I thought I might have made him suspicious. I sighed and told myself I had nothing to worry about, and neither did my mother. At least, I was pretty sure we had nothing to worry about.

Chapter six

I waited until I thought the detective had left the diner before emerging from the break room. Sam was at the grill and Luanne and another waitress, Georgia Johnson, were out front waiting tables. We had six waitresses, give or take, that worked various days and shifts. Which means sometimes Georgia and Carrie Aimes were a little flaky and would disappear for a few weeks at a time. Sam always took them back. He was good like that.

I strode over to Sam. "Why is that detective questioning everyone?" I hissed, putting my hands on my hips.

He continued flipping burgers without looking at me. "I guess it's his job."

I harrumphed. "Well, it seems like he could do his job by looking for whoever poisoned Celia and not harassing us. What is this world coming to when the people that tried to help Celia are being blamed for her death?"

He turned and looked at me with raised eyebrows. "He harassed you? Did he say you were a suspect? He only asked me a couple of questions about what happened that day."

I bit my lower lip. "I guess harassed is a strong word. But it seems odd that he came to talk to us again."

He shrugged. "He said he might be back by to talk to us the day Celia died. I think you're blowing this out of proportion."

"Am I? He brought up my mother, saying Celia was her only competition in town."

I probably *was* blowing things out of proportion, but my adrenaline had been triggered when I realized I was late to work, and then it skyrocketed when the detective wanted to talk to me. I was on a roll and I didn't have any breaks. I did things like that sometimes, but in my defense, I had felt uneasy ever since Celia's death. A killer was on the loose and who knew who might be next?

Sam turned back to the grill and flipped another burger. His hair was getting long and if he didn't get a haircut, he was going to have to wear a hair tie like the rest of us.

"Don't make a mountain out of an anthill or whatever it is people say. He just needs the facts and now that he's got them, I'm sure we won't hear from him again."

I sighed. "Fine."

He was right. I needed to pull myself together. There was no reason to be upset about all of this. The police would find the killer and that would be the end of this whole mess.

"Hey Rainey," Luanne said as she filled a glass with ice from the soft drink machine.

"Hey Luanne," I said and picked up an apron from the drawer where they were kept and tied it around my waist.

"That detective asked me about you and your mom," she said absently. "I told him I didn't think either of you were killers, but I've been known to be wrong before."

"What?" I nearly shouted. "He asked you if we were killers?"

"Yeah," she said with a shrug. "Don't worry. I got your back. Like I said, I told him I didn't think you would actually kill someone. Maybe cut close to someone in the crosswalk if they weren't going fast enough, but not out and out kill someone."

I closed the short distance between us. "Please tell me you're kidding."

She looked at me and thought for a moment. "No, I'm not kidding. I don't think either of you could kill someone. Not even if that someone was someone neither of you liked."

I groaned and headed back into the kitchen. "Did you hear that?"

Sam gave me a grin. "Don't pay attention to her. You know how confused Luanne gets. The detective didn't come in here wanting information about you and your mother specifically. In fact, I don't think he had anything more on his mind than making sure he understood what happened the day Celia died." The smile left his face, and he looked off into space a moment and then he turned back to the grill without another word. Sam had been acting a little off since Celia died and I didn't know what to make of it.

"Well, I don't need someone saying something that might lead him to believe there's even a hint of a possibility that I or my mother did something we didn't."

"Rainey, you're making more out of this than there is," he said again. "The tables are filling up out there. Can you help the girls take care of them?"

He had his back to me and I wanted to say more, but I had already been late to work and I didn't want to take advantage of his good nature like some of the other waitresses did.

"All right," I said and headed out front.

I was surprised to see my mother sitting at the counter. She smiled at me. "There's my little girl."

"Hey, Mom, what are you doing here?" I asked, heading over to her.

"I thought I'd have some of Sam's clam chowder. It's been ages since I've had some," she said and then leaned in closer to me. "It won't kill me, will it?"

I gasped. "Mom, don't say that!" I hissed.

She shrugged. "I know, I know. I met that new detective. He wanted to know if I knew anything about Celia's murder. It is a murder now, isn't it?"

"He questioned you?" I whispered. "He came to the shop and questioned you?" I thought that was going too far. My mother wasn't anywhere near Celia when she died.

She nodded. "Apparently someone told him I didn't like Celia, and that we argued a lot. That's just silly. We rarely argued. She gossiped about me and we tried to avoid each other whenever possible. Maybe I occasionally I told people her flowers were treated with cancerous chemicals, but that's it."

"Who told him you argued with her?" I asked, glancing up at the dining room. The place was filling up and if I didn't get in there and help, Georgia would whine to Sam.

"He wouldn't say. But he knew about an argument Celia and I had last year. You hadn't moved back home yet, but Celia insisted I was copying her flower arrangements. I wasn't. And besides, it's not like there's a copyright on floral arrangements. So, I confronted her when the rumors got back to me. Let's just say things didn't go well," she said. "Can I get some iced tea?"

"You had an argument over flower arrangements?" I asked. My mom didn't like to let things go. I shuddered, thinking how the argument must have gone.

She nodded. "It all started when she made a red, white, and blue flower arrangement in a red vase for the fourth of July. She added some flags and a blue teddy bear. I told her I had something similar in my shop. I had used a blue vase and a red teddy bear though. She flew off the handle, accusing me of copying her."

"Did you copy her?"

She looked at me wide-eyed. "I did not! I came up with the beary special patriotic arrangement all on my own."

"Okay, fine," I said. "Who do you think would tell the detective about the argument?"

"Like I said, he didn't tell me, but if I had to guess, I'd say it was her busybody friend, Patricia Cerner. The two of them were two peas in a pod. Each one just as nosy as the other," she said, nodding her head. "I'm really thirsty."

I leaned against the counter and thought about it. It did seem like something Patricia would do. She wasn't quite as obnoxious as Celia had been, but she had her moments. "You know what I'm going to do?"

"Get me some iced tea?"

"No. Yes, I'll get you some iced tea. But I'm going to see if I can do some snooping and see if I can dig up anything on Celia's death."

"Ooh!" she squealed. "That sounds like fun!"

"Shh," I said. "We need to keep this between the two of us."

"Do I get clam chowder?" she asked.

"Yeah, if you come back at lunchtime. You know we don't serve it until then."

"Hey, Rainey, are you going to do any work today?" Georgia called from the dining room. She had two empty plates in her hands and a sneer on her lips. "This ain't the Holiday Inn, you know. You've got to actually do some work around here."

I rolled my eyes. Georgia was so uncouth. "I'm on my way," I said over my shoulder. "I just need to get my customer some iced tea."

"She's not your customer, she's your mother," Georgia said, filling a tray with the plates and more dirty dishes from a now empty table.

"Hi Georgia," Mom said, waving at her.

Georgia snorted and I ignored her. It was better that way.

I headed to the soft drink machine, thinking about what my mother had said. If Patricia was spreading rumors, or worse, actually going to the detective and telling him my mother and I were suspicious, we could be in for some trouble. I had never gotten so much as a parking ticket. I didn't belong in jail. My only option was to find out who killed Celia Markson.

Chapter Seven

I was off work the next day and my mother was at the flower shop, so I had the house to myself if you didn't count the cat. Poofy was a long-haired orange tabby that liked to sleep on the windowsill or entwine herself between my feet when I walked. She was now soundly sleeping on the windowsill and I decided it was my chance to whip up something in the kitchen without danger of tripping and ending up face-first on the floor.

I missed cooking. Before the divorce, it had been something I did every day, but lately, my heart wasn't in it. That didn't mean I didn't miss it, it just meant I felt unable to really enjoy it.

I looked through the cupboards and refrigerator and decided on a blueberry tart. There was a bowl of the wonderful little berries on the kitchen counter, ripened to perfection. A neighbor grew them and had given us a small bucket full. They were so much tastier than the ones the grocery stores carried. These were firm and sweet and tasted of heaven.

I was primarily a baker, but I liked to cook, too. My favorite time of year was any time a holiday was near. Holidays gave me an excuse to cook to my heart's content. When I had cooked for the morning show in New York, I was given free rein to be as creative as I dared. I sighed, thinking back on those days. I missed the people from the morning show and I missed being on camera and explaining what I was doing as I whipped up something tasty.

I felt a nudge against my leg as I measured out flour for the crust.

"Well, good mid-morning, Poofy," I said. So much for being able to bake without tripping over her.

She purred in answer to me.

"I'm making a blueberry tart. I need you to take a step back so I can do this without tripping."

Meow.

"Your bowl is full," I pointed out to her.

Meow.

My mind went to Detective Starkey. He was a cocky know-it-all, and I didn't like him. And I really didn't like him looking in my mother's direction during the investigation. My mother wouldn't kill anyone. Annoy them with her smart-alecky mouth, maybe. But she was a good person. Even with Celia behaving hatefully toward her, she had almost always behaved herself in response. Almost.

Meow.

"Look in your bowl, Poofy."

I stepped around Poofy and got a medium-sized mixing bowl out of the cupboard and placed it by the sink. The blueberries were perfect. I gently poured some berries into the bowl and then ran it under the water to rinse them. Blueberries were one of my favorite fruits. Our neighbor had a dozen bushes that he babied and nursed all year long. The branches of the bushes were loaded with berries every spring and we reaped the benefits of his obsession.

The idea had occurred to me that I could try out some new recipes, bring them to the diner, and hopefully get some input from customers. Sam had a pretty basic menu that his customers had come to expect. Locally caught fish, plus lots of burgers, and his classic clam chowder. Clam chowder wasn't exactly a local dish, but Sam's was excellent and one of the most popular items on the menu. If I could slip in an occasional dessert or entrée, it would help me feel like I was doing the one thing I was put on this earth to do, and that was make wonderful food. I thought Sam would agree to it if I brought it up to him. I just hadn't done it yet.

I heard the front door open and a moment later Stormy appeared in the kitchen doorway.

"Hey," she said. "What are you doing?"

"Making blueberry tarts. What are you up to?" I asked as I mixed up a brown sugar topping to sprinkle over the tart.

"Lizzy gets out of preschool pretty soon, so I thought I'd stop by and say hi on my way to pick her up. Have you heard anything new about Celia's death?"

"I haven't heard much that's new, but that detective has questioned both me and Mom. It doesn't make any sense."

"Maybe he's just covering his bases. Chances are pretty good it was someone Celia knew. I think random murders are pretty rare unless you live in a big city."

"Yeah, I suppose he is," I said. "I'm going to figure out how to find the killer. I just haven't come up with a plan yet."

"Maybe you should just leave the investigation to the detective," she said hesitantly.

"You're probably right, but I'm probably not going to do that," I said and began creaming softened butter into the brown sugar and cinnamon I had just measured into the bowl.

She sighed. "That figures. I wonder if she had life insurance? She had a successful business. Maybe someone killed her over money."

"That's a good point. I wonder if there's a way to find out if she had life insurance," I said. The filling came together quickly, and I pressed the crust into the pan, poured the filling into it, and then sprinkled the topping over the tart. I had prepared a large one to take to the diner and a smaller one for my mother and me for dessert.

"It's worth researching," she said. "You can find out almost anything on the internet, but I would think life insurance policies would be kept private."

"Probably so," I agreed. There had to be a way to find out more about Celia. I needed to find her killer. I had already searched the internet, but all I came up with was a yellow pages ad for her business and an old Facebook page that looked like it hadn't been updated in several years.

I slipped the blueberry tarts into the oven and soon the house smelled wonderfully sweet as they baked. Stormy left to pick up her youngest daughter, Lizzy, and I sat on the couch with Poofy in my lap and an old black and white mystery on the television.

A CUSTOMER HELD OPEN the door to the diner for me as I carried the larger blueberry tart inside. The noontime rush had cleared out, and I figured Sam and the girls would welcome a treat. Plus, it was a bribe to get Sam to agree to let me try out my recipes on the customers.

"Hey, Georgia, Luanne, Diane," I said as I passed them and headed to the kitchen. "Hey, Sam."

He looked up from scraping the grill. "Hey, Rainey. What are you doing here? It's your day off."

I set the tart down on the counter. "I was in a baking mood, so I thought I would bring you the fruits of my labor. Pun intended." I went to the cupboard and took down some dessert plates and then got some forks from a drawer.

He put down the wire brush he was using to clean the grill and came to look at the tart. "That does look good."

"It's wonderful, if I do say so myself."

"What do you have there?" Luanne asked, peering over my shoulder.

"A blueberry tart." I cut pieces for everyone as the other girls wandered into the kitchen from the dining room. I topped the slices with a bit of whipped cream from the fridge.

After everyone had taken a bite or two, there were groans of appreciation all around. It made me smile. Sam served dessert at the diner, but it was usually store-bought pies and cakes. The tart was something a little more special than what he usually served.

"I can see why you were on that television show," Sam said around a mouthful of tart.

"You know, Sam, I was thinking. Maybe we could come up with a plan to serve desserts like this here at the diner."

"A plan?" he asked and shoved another bite of tart into his mouth.

I nodded. "Yeah, a plan. Why buy pies and cakes from the store? I've got an idea for a new cookbook. I could try out my new recipes here at the diner and see how the customers like them. That would give me feedback and ideas to tweak my recipes and help me create a better cookbook."

He narrowed his eyes at me. "Tired of waitressing?"

I shrugged. "I wouldn't say tired of it. Well okay, maybe a little. It just seems like a waste of my talents."

Georgia snorted.

I shot her a look and turned back to Sam. "I think it would draw in more customers. Or, at the very least, make your current customers happier than they already are. Maybe you could supply some of the ingredients and in return, you get new menu items to offer the customers."

"I don't know," Sam said doubtfully and took another bite.

"Why not?" I asked, trying not to whine.

"I think it's a great idea," Luanne volunteered.

"Thanks, Luanne," I said. Sometimes Luanne came in handy, like now when I needed support to get Sam to agree to my idea.

"You aren't that great of a waitress. You always forget to bring the customers something and they complain," Luanne added. "They wouldn't miss you being out on the floor that much."

I turned and glared at her.

She shrugged and went back to eating her tart.

"You don't have to make a decision now," I told Sam. "But maybe it's something we can discuss. And don't listen to Luanne. She doesn't know what she's talking about."

Sam grinned at me. "The customers like you just fine. But sometimes you do forget things."

I sighed. "Okay, I'll work harder at making sure I get everything out to the tables."

"We can talk about it," Sam said and finished up his piece of tart. "You're going to leave the rest of that here, aren't you?"

"Sure, I can leave the rest of it here. You like it, right?"

"It's pretty tasty. A lot better than those pies I buy at the store. But if you're going to be baking all the time, that leaves me short a waitress."

"I don't have to quit waitressing. Not at first, anyway. Maybe we can try a new entrée or dessert a couple times a week and see how it goes."

"I'll think about it," he said and set his plate next to the sink.

"Where's Ron?" I asked, noticing our dishwasher wasn't around and the sink was piled with dirty dishes.

He shrugged. "Called in sick. We'll be here late getting those washed. Unless you'd like to step in and give us a hand?"

I frowned. I really wanted to go home and spend some time doing nothing. "Sure," I said reluctantly. Maybe if I helped out now, he would accept my business proposal.

Chapter Eight

After getting Sam's promise that he would consider my business proposal, and washing more dishes than I have ever washed in my life, I said my goodbyes and headed for the front door. Sam followed me to lock the door behind me.

"You sure you don't want to stay and finish the rest of the dishes?" he asked me.

"Nope. There's not much left and I'm going home to enjoy the rest of my day off."

"Okay, well, your loss then," he joked.

Before I could get to the front door, it swung open and Celia's boyfriend, Gerald Vance, blocked the doorway. Gerald stood nearly six-feet-five-inches tall and was a formidable presence.

"You!" he said, pointing over my shoulder at Sam.

I took a step back and glanced at Sam.

"What's going on, Gerald?" Sam asked, putting one hand in his front jeans pocket. He looked a little nervous as he looked up at Gerald.

"What did you do to my Celia? The cops said you poisoned her!"

I gasped. I could smell a hint of alcohol mixed with peppermint coming from Gerald's direction and his face was red with rage. He was a lot older than Sam, but he was also a lot bigger with Sam coming in at five-feet nine-inches. I could sense the other girls coming up behind us and I wondered if we could all take him down if we needed to.

"Now Gerald, I'm sure if the police thought I killed Celia they would have arrested me," Sam said, sounding calmer than I thought he was. His face had gone white.

CLAM CHOWDER AND A MURDER 59

"You did kill her!" Gerald insisted, sticking a big meaty finger in Sam's face.

"Gerald, I think you need to calm down," I said. I didn't want to see Sam punched in the face and with the anger rolling off Gerald, I thought it was a real possibility.

"Don't tell me to calm down when my Celia's gone," he said, his voice cracked when he said her name.

Adrenaline surged through my body and I took a deep breath. There were tears in Gerald's eyes and I felt terrible for him, but he had no business accusing Sam of something as terrible as murder.

"Gerald, I'm sorry for your loss. I really am. Celia was a regular customer here and she'll be missed," Sam said quietly. "I'm sure the police are working hard to figure out what happened."

"And you know there's always the possibility it wasn't a murder," I pointed out. "The detective said they haven't gotten the toxicology report back yet."

He turned to me. "Why is the detective talking to you? Are you the one that poisoned Celia? You did it? I always thought you were a nice person, Rainey Daye!"

"What? No. No, I didn't do anything. The detective was here asking us about what happened the day Celia died. That's all. He said he just wanted to make sure he knew what happened."

"I bet it was your mother then," he said, curling his hands into fists. "I bet your mother had something to do with it, didn't she? Celia always said your mother harassed her and tried to steal her customers." He stood up straighter, jutting his chin out. Gerald had white hair that stuck up on the sides and his beige long sleeve shirt had come untucked from his jeans. He looked a bit like a madman.

"My mother didn't do anything to Celia, and she never tried to steal anyone's customers." It was as ridiculous to think my mother had anything to do with Celia's death, as it was to think she had tried to steal her customers. It was the other way around. Celia had tried to steal my mother's customers.

He narrowed his eyes at me and then turned back to Sam. "I'm going to talk to that detective again. You wait and see. If anyone here had anything to do with my Celia's death, you're going to regret it." He looked at each of us for emphasis and then spun around with a surprising amount of finesse for someone his size and left the diner, letting the door slam hard behind him.

"Can you believe that?" Luanne said. "He's nuts if he thinks anyone here had anything to do with Celia's death."

Sam hurried to the diner door and locked it, then turned around to face us. "Okay, here's the thing. We need to not speak to anyone about this. I mean it. The last thing I need is for it to spread that we had something to do with poisoning Celia Markson. Gerald's got a big mouth and I'm sure he'll tell people."

"People are probably already talking about it," Luanne said. "News spreads fast around here, and everyone knows she died in our parking lot."

"Could it have been food poisoning?" Georgia asked. "I mean, it could have been an accident."

"I doubt food poisoning could kill that fast and besides that, she had heartburn when she came in. She didn't seem herself," I pointed out. "I'm sure whatever it was, it began before she got here."

"It doesn't matter what she died of, we had nothing to do with it," Sam said and then headed back toward the kitchen.

"I hope Gerald goes home and sleeps this off. I smelled alcohol," I said to the girls. "He's always been kind of crazy, so maybe no one will believe him if he does try to spread it around that we poisoned Celia."

Georgia nodded. "I could smell alcohol from over here. That Celia Markson was a pain in everyone's behind. She died. Who cares? He'll get over it."

I rolled my eyes. Georgia was also a pain. "The police care and obviously Gerald does. Besides, doesn't it mean anything to you that someone died?"

She crossed her arms over her ample chest and shook her head. "Nope."

I shook my head at her. "I have to go. Can you lock the door behind me?" I turned back to the door and unlocked it to let myself out.

"Sure," Georgia said, following me to the door. "I hope Gerald isn't hiding out there in the parking lot waiting for you."

"Gee, thanks, Georgia," I said and headed out the door. The parking lot was nearly empty, and I didn't see Gerald anywhere. I let out a sigh of relief and headed to my car.

I felt my phone vibrate, and I pulled it out of my jeans pocket to read the text.

Rainey, I've been arrested for killing Celia. Can you post my bail?

Mom

Chapter Nine

CLAM CHOWDER AND A MURDER

My heart pounded in my chest as I sped to the police station. *What on earth happened?*

My mother was no killer, but she sometimes didn't care what came out of her mouth. It wouldn't surprise me if she had told Detective Cade Starkey that she was glad Celia was dead. And since the detective needed a suspect, my mother would be a convenient one.

I parked my car and jumped out, heading for the front door of the police station. How would I get her out of this mess? My mind was spinning with questions. Innocent people went to jail every day, and I needed to keep my mom from being one of them.

"Hi, I need to speak to someone about my mother, Mary Ann Daye. She was arrested today," I said, to the woman behind the front desk. I tried to steady my breathing, but with my heart pounding in my chest, I sounded like I had just run a mile.

She narrowed her eyes at me and then turned to her computer without a word. Tapping on the keyboard, she peered at her computer screen, and then looked up. "I don't have anything on her in my computer. Sometimes processing takes a while. You can have a seat and wait." She motioned toward a row of orange plastic chairs connected by a steel frame beneath them.

I held up my phone. "She texted me and said she was arrested. How do I know what's going on with her? Is there someone I can speak to right now? I can't just wait and let her sit in a jail cell." I tried to keep the panic out of my voice, but I had a feeling I wasn't very successful.

The woman began to roll her eyes but caught herself and shook her head. "If your mother was arrested, she would not have been allowed to keep her cell phone. Why don't you call her and ask her what's going on?"

I felt my face go pink. Of course, she wouldn't have been allowed to keep her phone. Why hadn't I thought to call her first?

"Oh," I said, nodding. "Sure."

I stepped back from the front desk as a woman that had just entered the building stepped up to speak with the woman behind the desk. I hit dial and waited for my mother to pick up.

"Hello Rainey," she said, not sounding the least bit distressed.

I sighed. "Mom, where are you?"

"I'm at the police station. Are you coming to bail me out?"

"Mom, if you were arrested, why would you have your cell phone? They wouldn't let you keep that! What's going on?" I hissed into the phone and turned my back on the two women at the desk. Sometimes I didn't think things through and this was one of those times.

"Are you coming to get me?"

"I'm here now, but you have not been arrested according to the woman at the front desk. What's going on?" I asked again.

"I'm being interrogated by the detective," she said, sounding matter-of-fact. "It's terribly cold in this room and the lights are bright. It's inhumane."

I heard a muffled chuckle that sounded distinctly male. "Mom, I don't have time for this. Tell me what's really going on."

"The detective is coming out to meet you. He'll fill you in," she said. "I'm going to hang up now."

I hit end just as Detective Starkey entered the reception room from a side door. He had a smile on his face and I wanted to wipe it off for him. I felt like a fool for panicking.

"Ms. Daye," he said. "Would you like to come on back to visit awhile? We have coffee and donuts, although I'm pretty sure they're both at least a day old."

I took a deep breath and crossed the room to him. "What's going on? Why is my mother being interrogated?"

"Your mother is a delightful woman, but she has not been arrested, nor is she being interrogated. I called her and asked if she would come down so we can have a few words with her, but I assure you she has not been arrested." He kept smiling, and I really had to control myself to keep from saying something I would regret. The man infuriated me.

"Delightful? I don't call it delightful when she texts me and tells me she's been arrested! Do you know what I've been through the last, well, the last fifteen minutes?" I could feel my face getting hotter, and I took a deep breath to try and calm down.

"I can only imagine. But I assure you, she's fine, and she hasn't been arrested. In fact, her car is out in the parking lot and she's free to go anytime. Currently, she's regaling some of the other officers and myself with tales of her twin daughters' escapades in the fifth grade. Something about pretending to be one another so the twin without a boyfriend could get her first kiss with her sister's boyfriend."

I gasped as that memory rushed back to me. At eleven, none of my friends had a real boyfriend, but Stormy had insisted that Davey Smith was her boyfriend and made him kiss her. Then, since I didn't have a boyfriend, Stormy insisted I pretend I was her and the rest was history. It wasn't a moment I was proud of. Mom wouldn't have known about it, but when I did have my first boyfriend, Stormy told her I had already had my first kiss. Stormy still needed to learn to shut her mouth.

"You know what? I think I'll be on my way. I must have missed my mother's car in the parking lot, but since it's here, you'll tell her she's on her own, won't you?" I spun around and headed for the door without waiting for his reply.

"No problem," he called as I pushed open the front door.

My mother. I loved her, but she had a way of embarrassing me like no one else could. It wasn't until I was in my car and driving down the street that I wondered why my mother was being questioned again.

Chapter Ten

After I left the police station, I stopped in at the British Tea and Coffee Company. I needed a dose of sweet caffeine to help me settle down. The British Tea and Coffee Company was a cute shop filled with everything British in tea, coffee, candy, and baked goods. The shop was owned by my friend, Agatha Broome. She was a British transplant and seemed to always have a tale to tell, and it was one of my favorite places to relax.

When I entered the shop, Agatha and Donna Jones, my mother's assistant at the flower shop, were sitting at a table, their heads close together.

"Hello, Agatha! Hello, Donna!" I called, putting a smile on my face that I didn't feel. The day was wearing on me. First, I had spent a significant part of my day off washing dishes and then the encounter with Gerald Vance. Not to mention my mother crying wolf and another encounter with Detective Cade Starkey that left me feeling yet again that there was something about him that I just didn't like.

"Oh, hello, Rainey," Agatha said in her crisp English accent. "How are you this afternoon?"

"I'm great," I said, deciding not to dwell on what felt like a wasted day. "I need my daily dose of caffeine." I headed to the front counter to place my order.

I decided on a large vanilla latte with an extra shot of espresso, and then headed for a table in the corner.

"Rainey," Donna said and waved me over.

I joined them at their table instead and took a seat. I wanted to unload about Gerald but decided it wasn't the right thing to do. The man was grieving and who was to say I wouldn't have done the same thing? No, I probably wouldn't have, but still. I didn't want to gossip about it.

Donna leaned in. "Have you heard anything new about Celia's murder?"

I shook my head and took a sip of my latte. "No, as far as I know, it's still under investigation."

"It's been the talk of the town," Agatha said, nodding. "She was a pesky gossip, but it's a terrible thing that happened to her." Her accent was still clean and crisp even though she hadn't lived in England for more than two decades.

"I guess we don't get much excitement around here," I agreed. "I just hope they find whoever did it and put them away. Actually, I'm wondering if they might ultimately decide her death was from natural causes. That would be the best possible development, if you want to know the truth." Even though it didn't seem probable, I was still holding out hope for this scenario.

"Oh, I agree," Agatha said. "I hate the idea that there's a killer on the loose. It doesn't make me feel safe." Agatha had short, curly white hair and wore gold-framed glasses. She looked like everyone's favorite grandma.

Donna nodded and glanced around the room. "Me too. Did you see the paper?"

I shook my head as Donna slipped a newspaper in front of me that was folded over and opened to the lifestyle section. There was a quarter page ad in script font addressed to Celia.

To the love of my life, Celia Markson,
I loved you from the minute I laid eyes on you.
There has never been anyone else for me

since the day you smiled at me and said hello.
You'll be missed more than words can say.
I'm sorry I couldn't be more of what you needed.
Please forgive me. You deserved so much more.
Your loving man, Gerald Vance.

"Wow," I said. "Poor Gerald." The message was encircled with hearts and flowers and was touching in an awkward way.

"Yes, poor Gerald," Agatha agreed. "I didn't realize they were as serious as all that. I heard Celia and Gerald had broken up, but I guess they got back together before she passed."

"Really? I guess I'm out of the loop on things like that," I said and took a sip of my coffee. If Celia had broken up with Gerald, it was news to me.

She nodded. "Celia said she had found the perfect man in Gerald, then about a month or so ago, she said they broke up, but she didn't say why." She shrugged. "I guess they patched things up."

"I was talking to your mother today, Rainey," Donna said with a grin. "We both wondered if they might discover Celia died of natural causes. Otherwise, your mother might be in trouble." She looked at Agatha and they both laughed.

"What? What do you mean?" I asked looking from one to the other.

"Sorry, Rainey. I'm just kidding. I did tell your mom that she better have a good excuse for where she was the day Celia died, otherwise they might haul her in," Donna said and laughed again.

"What do you mean?" I repeated. "She was at work when Celia died." My mind went back to that day. Mom was home by the time I got there, but she had said she was at the flower shop earlier that day.

"No," she said hesitantly. "That was the day she called me and said she wasn't going to come in. she said she had some errands to run and asked if Jana and I could handle the shop that day."

I stared at her. Was I making a mistake? Had Mom said she worked earlier that day or was I remembering incorrectly?

"Oh," I said, nodding my head. "That's right. I completely forgot." My mind was blank. Hadn't she said she was at work? I needed to have a talk with her when I got home.

"There was a lot of excitement that day. Of course, you forgot," Agatha said helpfully. "I'm sure you had your mind on other things."

I nodded. "Yeah, it was quite a shock discovering Celia's body."

"I can't imagine how hard that must have been," Agatha said, patting my hand. "It would put me in shock for a good long while."

I nodded again and racked my brain to remember the conversation my mother and I had had. If she wasn't at work, then certainly she had a good reason not to go in that day. Not that it even mattered. My mother may not be especially grieved that Celia had died, but she couldn't hurt anyone. It was ridiculous to even think otherwise. I shook off the sick feeling in the pit of my stomach and took another sip of my latte.

"HI HONEY," MOM SAID when she came through the front door.

"Hi Mom, how was your day?" I asked, removing the roasted chicken from the oven. I had stuffed the cavity with carrots, potatoes, and onions and slipped slivered garlic cloves and fresh basil leaves beneath the skin before popping it into the oven. I had basted it twice with the drippings while it cooked and the house smelled wonderfully delicious and cozy.

I had had time to calm down and decided not to jump all over her about the text she had sent me earlier. I'd deal with that later.

"Wow, that makes my stomach growl. It smells really good," she said, coming into the kitchen and inhaling deeply. "What's for dessert?"

"I made blueberry tarts. I took one to the diner for Sam and the girls to try. I would love to be able to bake desserts and maybe even an entrée or two to try out new recipes and serve them at the diner. I'm thinking about writing a new cookbook." I was holding back on asking where she was on the day Celia died. I didn't want her to think I didn't believe her when she told me she had been at work that day.

"You're so good to me," she said. "I'm going to kick my shoes off and enjoy dinner with my lovely daughter. Sounds like a heavenly evening."

"So, what was the deal with the police station?" I asked casually.

"Oh, that nice detective called and asked me to come down to the station. He wondered when the last time was that I had seen Celia and whether I had seen or heard anything that might be helpful in the investigation," she said off-handedly. "Sorry I worried you. We thought it would be fun to tease you about my being arrested."

"We? Really Mom? You thought it would be fun? You have a decidedly odd sense of fun," I said, exasperated. So much for keeping my cool. "Why did he question you about the murder again? Doesn't it worry you that he keeps talking to you about it?"

She shrugged. "Why should it? I didn't kill Celia. I'm perfectly innocent. I even asked him if he thought I was the killer. Do you know what he said?"

I stared at her, then sighed. Only my mother would ask the detective that question. "No, what?"

"He asked if I did kill her. I laughed and told him he was silly. He agreed with me. I'm going to go kick my shoes off, dear. I'll be right back." She headed off to her bedroom, humming as she went.

I sighed. How could she remain calm in the face of police questioning? I put the vegetables and the chicken on a serving plate and carried it to the table. Poofy began madly encircling my legs and meowing.

"You'll have to wait your turn," I told her.

"Poofy, come into the bedroom," Mom said emerging from her room. She picked the cat up and took her into her room and closed the door. Poofy always insisted that she taste whatever we ate, and it was safer to put her behind closed doors until we finished dinner. She would get her share of roast chicken later.

"Besides being questioned by the police yet again, how was your day?" I asked Mom as we sat down. I helped myself to the chicken and potatoes.

"Oh, you know how it is. Flowers are flowers. Ironically I've sold a few arrangements for Celia's funeral. I would have thought they would buy them from her shop. But, I'm not going to turn anyone away. Money is money."

"That's kind of odd, don't you think? Buying flowers for Celia's funeral from her competition?" I said, cutting into a potato with my fork. "I hope the police figure out who killed Celia."

"I know. I can't imagine who did it," she said. "So you're going to write a new cookbook? Do you think anyone would publish it? Don't you have a black eye in the publishing world? That ex-husband of yours seemed relentless in destroying your career."

I looked at her, stunned. "No, I don't have a black eye. Just because my last publisher dropped me doesn't mean another publisher won't pick me up. Craig doesn't control every publisher in New York."

It was something I had been trying not to think about. My ex-husband had lied about me and damaged my reputation, but he only had influence at one publishing house. It would be fine. I hoped.

"Good. I was afraid you had lost your nerve about publishing another book. You're a fabulous cook and baker and you need to write another book."

I breathed a sigh of relief. For a moment I thought she might believe I couldn't do it. My own belief was weak; I needed someone to believe in me.

"Mom, did you take the day off from work the day Celia was killed?" I asked nonchalantly.

She looked at me. "No, I was there most of the day. I did come home early to put that roast on, but I was there. Why do you ask?"

I shrugged. "I don't know. I guess I've had this whole murder thing on my mind a lot. How many times has the detective talked to you?" I had hoped I was remembering things wrong, but here she was, repeating what she had already told me.

She shrugged. "I suppose it's been a couple of times. He doesn't seem to have much information on what happened."

"Did he ask you where you were the day Celia died? It seems weird that he's talked to you a couple of times."

She looked up at me. "Why, Rainey, do you think I had something to do with Celia's death?"

"No, of course not," I said, with a laugh that sounded as phony as a three-dollar bill. "I just hate that the detective has talked to both of us. It seems like his time could be better spent looking for the killer."

She nodded. "That's the truth. He's wasting his time talking to either of us, but I suppose he's doing what he feels he needs to do."

I looked at her as she ate. Why wouldn't she tell me the truth? Or was it Donna that wasn't telling the truth? But if so, why would Donna say Mom wasn't at the shop if she was? Something didn't add up.

Chapter Eleven

"Good morning, Rainey," Cade Starkey said when I stepped into the diner.

I had a cup of designer coffee in one hand and a pan of apple blueberry cinnamon rolls in the other. My face dropped. He was sitting at the diner counter, a half-eaten plate of scrambled eggs, bacon, and toast in front of him. The shine in his hair was blinding beneath the fluorescent lights and he looked dashing in his black suit, as usual. Not that I noticed things like that.

I stopped in my tracks and stared, mouth open. I can be dashing too, just not at that particular moment. "Good morning," I said when I had recovered my composure.

"Good Morning, Rainey," Carlisle Garlock said from his corner seat at the counter. He had his usual breakfast in front of him. A cup of black coffee and a short stack of pancakes.

"Good morning, Carlisle," I said, smiling.

"How are you on this lovely morning, Ms. Daye?" Cade asked as I headed toward the kitchen.

"I'm great. I didn't expect to see you here," I said without slowing down. I didn't wait for a response from him.

When I entered the kitchen, Sam turned to look at me as I set the pan of cinnamon rolls down on the counter. "Good morning," he said with a grin on his face.

"I brought some apple blueberry cinnamon rolls. Maybe we can try them out on the customers? I can put them in a display case out front."

He nodded. "Sure. Go ahead."

"Great. We can give out samples and see if we can sell some. Maybe I can get some customer opinions on them."

I headed to the break room to put my purse in a locker and then back to the kitchen. The cinnamon rolls were stuffed with apple and blueberry filling and smothered in cream cheese frosting. They had been featured on one morning show last summer. I had wanted to bake up another pan of them before now, but it hadn't happened. When I found myself unable to sleep at 3:00 a.m., I got out of bed and started working on the dough. Now was the perfect time to make them again. This time I added more cardamom to the filling.

I glanced through the pass-through and saw Cade Starkey watching me. I looked down again without acknowledging him. He made me nervous. I filled the glass cake stand with cinnamon rolls and then cut some into sample size chunks. I inserted a toothpick into each chunk and put them into a covered dish.

When I was satisfied with my work, I carried the cake stand and the sample dish out front.

"Those look good," Cade said, eyeing the cake stand.

"They are good. Would you like to try a sample?"

"I certainly would," he said, leaning toward the samples and giving them the eye.

I set the cake stand down and lifted the lid to the sample dish. He reached in and picked up a wooden toothpick with cinnamon roll attached and ate the pastry.

"Wow," he said, closing his eyes for a second. "That is really good. Did you make them?"

I nodded, trying not to look too pleased with his praise. "I bake a little." There was no reason for me to think he might know who I was. Sure, I'd had three cookbooks on the New York Times bestseller list in the past five years, and I'd had the gig with the morning show, but few people outside of New York knew me by sight, even if they had heard of my cookbooks. It had been a dream of mine to get a show on the Food Network, but that was also the dream of a lot of other bakers and cooks. I never heard anything back on the demos I sent them.

"Mmm...they're great. Can I get one?" he asked.

"Sure," I said without looking at him. I got a dessert plate and a clean fork out of the cupboard behind the counter and put a cinnamon roll on the plate, placing it in front of him.

"Thanks," he said while I refilled his coffee cup. "I'll probably regret it, but I can't pass it up."

"I hope you like it," I said, trying not to sound too friendly.

"I'm sure I will."

I picked up a dishcloth and started wiping down the front counter, keeping one eye on him. "So, have you heard anything new about Celia's murder?" I asked, trying to sound casual.

"We've been investigating, but haven't found anything significant. I've talked to a lot of people and no one seems to know much of anything. Of course, that isn't surprising. But someone obviously disliked her enough to kill her and killers usually give themselves away, eventually. Something will turn up."

I nodded. "It's a small town. Someone has to know something." I regretted it as soon as it was out of my mouth. It sounded like *I* knew something. There was still a small part of me that hoped the medical examiner would say he'd made a mistake and she really died of a stroke.

"I'm sure someone does," he said and looked up from his cinnamon roll. "I do hear a lot about your mother and Celia not getting along. I guess that might be expected since they had businesses that competed with one another. Still, it seems there was a lot of animosity between the two of them."

I looked at him and willed myself not to look shocked. The fact that my mother hadn't told me the truth about where she had been on the day Celia died crossed my mind. My mother wasn't a killer. At least, I was relatively certain she wasn't. She probably had a perfectly good reason not to tell me the truth. Unless...she had flipped out and murdered Celia on a whim. I shook myself. Thinking those kinds of thoughts would drive me mad.

"What do you mean, animosity? Who said there was animosity?" I asked, trying to sound casual.

He shrugged. "That's just the talk around town. Of course, sometimes people embellish, especially when one of the people being talked about has been murdered."

He watched me closely as he spoke. I forced myself to smile. "It's a small town. People talk whether they actually know anything or not."

"Like I said, people could be embellishing. What about you?"

"What? What about me?" I felt my eyes go wide, and I forced myself to try to look relaxed instead of verging on freaked out, which is what I really felt.

"What do you think happened?"

I stared at him. Was he trying to trick me into saying something incriminating?

"I think someone killed Celia because she was a mean, hateful person. But I don't think it was my mother. My mother doesn't have a mean bone in her body. Are you trying to say my mother murdered Celia Markson?" I narrowed my eyes at him. He may have intimidated me, but I wasn't going to cower before him.

He sat back on his stool and held up his hands with his palms toward me. "Whoa. I am not saying anything of the sort. I was just wondering if you had any ideas about what happened."

"Really? Because it sounds like you're trying to say something without coming out and saying it," I said, putting my hands on my hips. I'd been in New York just long enough to not be afraid to stand up for myself. Before I moved there I had been a little on the shy side, but for the most part, that was gone.

"I am not saying anything of the sort. Don't jump to conclusions," he said and picked up his fork again. "I'm sure you'd tell me if you knew something, right?"

"Of course I'd tell you if I knew something. I don't want a killer wandering the streets of Sparrow."

He nodded. "I can appreciate that. This is a great cinnamon roll."

I nodded and turned away. My glance went to the pass-through window and I saw Sam watching us intently. His face was pale and when he saw me looking at him, he turned back to the grill. Sam hadn't seemed himself since Celia had died. It was probably because her last meal had been eaten in his diner.

"You gonna get something done today?" Georgia said loudly from the dining room entrance.

It brought me out of my thoughts and I nodded and tied an apron around my waist.

Chapter Twelve

I thought all day about my encounter with the detective. His words didn't match what his eyes were telling me. He may have said he didn't think my mother had anything to do with Celia's murder, but I wasn't sure it was the truth. My mother wasn't the murdering type. Sure, she hadn't told me the truth about where she had been, but there had to be a reason for that. My mother wasn't ordinarily a liar.

When night fell, I changed into all black clothes and donned gloves and a knit hat. It was time to put action to my words and see if I could find some information about Celia and her death. The killer had to have left clues behind. Mom had gone to her room to read before bed, so I was in the clear. I tiptoed across the living room and was reaching for the doorknob when the hall light came on.

"Rainey Jane, where are you going?" Mom asked.

I gasped and stopped in my tracks. "Going? I'm not going anywhere," I said, looking over my shoulder. Poofy rubbed against my leg and meowed. I needed to plan my getaways more carefully.

"Really? Because you've got your purse over your shoulder and you're reaching for the front doorknob. Call me crazy, but it looks like you're going somewhere."

I sighed and turned toward her. "I'm just going for a drive," I said, trying to think up a good excuse. "A drive to get a milkshake. Yeah, I need a milkshake."

She narrowed her eyes at me. "A milkshake? At eight o'clock? It's too late to drink that many calories. You'll never burn them off."

I shrugged. "You know how it is. I got a hankering for a chocolate milkshake and darned if my hankerings can tell time."

"I don't believe you. You've never used the word 'hankering' before. Tell me where you're going." She put her hands on her hips and eyed me like she used to when cookies disappeared from the cookie jar. I usually blamed Stormy, but it had been me most of the time. Even back then, I had a sweet tooth that dictated my actions.

I stared back. "Tell me where you were the day Celia died. And don't tell me you were at work. Donna already told me you called in." I'm not proud of myself for bringing it up like that, but there it was.

Her eyes opened wide. "It's none of your business," she said, raising her chin in defiance.

"Oh, really? Well, I know a certain detective that would like to know that little tidbit of information. It's lucky for you that Donna thinks you're a good employer or she might be the one to spill the beans to him."

She rolled her eyes. "That detective is nosy. He doesn't need to know my business. And there's no way Donna would squeal. She loves me. She said I was the best boss she ever had."

"Mom, where were you?" I asked. "Why did you tell me you were at work?"

"Do you think I killed Celia?"

"Of course not! But why wouldn't you tell me the truth? I'm your daughter!"

"Because some things are just private," she said, relaxing her stance.

Private?

CLAM CHOWDER AND A MURDER

"Oh my gosh. You aren't sick, are you? Are you sick Mom? Do you have cancer?" My father had died of skin cancer and I suddenly had visions of my mother wasting away in a hospital bed.

"No, I'm not sick. But I don't think it's your business." She took two steps toward me and stopped, folding her arms across her chest.

"Promise me you aren't sick," I begged and went to her.

"I'm not sick, but I did see a doctor," she said, looking at the floor.

"Why would you see a doctor if you aren't sick?" I asked as Poofy pawed my leg for attention. I reached down and scratched her ear, then straightened up again.

She looked at me. "Promise you can keep a secret?"

"I promise."

"I went to see a plastic surgeon," she said and looked away again.

"What? A plastic surgeon? For what?"

"I'm sagging," she hissed.

"What's sagging? What are you talking about?" She wasn't making any sense.

She glanced at her chest. "Now, tell me where you're going."

"That's ridiculous. You're only fifty-seven. You're fine. You don't need plastic surgery," I said, trying to make sense of this. "Why would you want to keep that a secret?"

"Because no one from my generation admits to plastic surgery, but everyone has it done. We just don't talk about it," she said, nodding. "Now, where are you going? Stop changing the subject."

"I'm not changing the subject, and I'm going for a drive," I said and headed back toward the door.

"Rainey, talk to me."

"Okay, fine. I'm going to have a look around Celia's house." It was a dumb idea, I know. It's not like I could get into the house and what would I discover from looking around the yard? I doubted much of anything, but I was going stir crazy thinking about the detective looking closely at my mother.

"Oh, good. I've wanted to do that. Let's go," she said and picked her purse up from the sofa. "Celia always bragged about spending all her money on expensive furniture and artwork. I want to see it. Artwork. Please. What a waste of money." She rolled her eyes and headed to the front door.

"What? You can't go with me. You're a suspect," I insisted.

"Suspect, shmuspect. I haven't done anything wrong, and I had a doctor's appointment to prove I have an alibi. Besides, you're the one that may have served her poisoned clam chowder. Let's go." She pushed past me, opened the front door, and headed to my car.

I sighed. My mother was going to get me into trouble if I wasn't careful.

Chapter Thirteen

Celia lived three blocks up and two streets over from my mother's house. The house was an eye-catching English cottage style. It was cute, and I'd heard Celia liked to collect antiques so I expected the inside of the house to match the outside. She visited the British Tea and Coffee Company frequently, bragging about the authentic English antiques she had imported from Britain. Agatha was never impressed. After all, she'd lived it.

I parked a block away, and we got out and walked. Celia's house was dark, and the drapes were closed. As I unlatched the wrought iron gate and pushed it open, I wondered who would handle the estate. The gate protested with a loud creak.

"Shh," Mom hissed from behind me.

"I'm trying," I said, pushing it open wider.

"Seems like Celia should have been able to afford some oil to grease those hinges," Mom sniffed.

"Seems like it," I said, leading the way to the front porch.

"What are we looking for?" she whispered.

"I don't know," I said, looking over my shoulder and then down the street. If we got caught here, I didn't know how we would explain ourselves. The detective already had his eye on my mother, and possibly me. He wouldn't buy that we were trying to help him with the investigation.

We tiptoed carefully up the front porch steps and I looked over my shoulder and down the street again. A dog barked in the distance and I hoped neither of Celia's neighbors owned dogs. We'd be in deep trouble if they did and they started barking.

"Seems like Celia could have painted the exterior of her house. The paint's chipping a little around the window," Mom observed, leaning in closer to the window in the dark.

"I wish you would have worn black," I said. Her white t-shirt practically glowed in the dark.

"Next time give me some notice that we're going to sneak around in the dark and do something illegal, and I'll wear all black just like you are. By the way, you're going to have trouble explaining that getup to the detective if we get caught."

I snorted and walked the length of the porch. I was feeling silly for even being here. What did we hope to find? Probably nothing worthwhile.

"Are we going to go inside?"

"Sure, Mom, just as soon as I find a key," I said, my words dripping with sarcasm.

"You mean, like this one?" she said holding a key out to me in the dark.

"What? What's that?" I asked squinting my eyes and coming toward her.

"A key."

"To Celia's house? Where did you find that?" The woman never ceased to amaze me.

"Under the doormat. Donna's sister dog sits for Celia and she keeps a key under the mat for her," she said inserting the key into the lock. "Just something you pick up in conversation."

"Oh, boy," I said. "I wonder where the dog is now. Wait, if we go in, we can get arrested for breaking and entering."

"It's trespassing, not breaking and entering. Or maybe just entering, I don't know. And what did we come here for, if not to go inside?" she asked, turning the knob. "Hopefully someone has the dog. I'd hate for him to be alone in the house."

"Me too," I said and looked over my shoulder once more before following her into the house. I pulled the door closed behind me and peered into the darkness.

"It's stuffy in here," she said, sniffing.

"I have a small flashlight," I said and pulled it out of my pocket. The house was neat and clean as I swept the light around the living room.

"Be careful," she said, pushing my hand down. "We don't want anyone to see the light."

"The drapes are drawn, we're fine," I said and walked further into the room. The sofas were trimmed in what looked like hand-carved mahogany. The cushions were overstuffed and looked comfy and inviting. I wanted to sink into them.

"What are we looking for?" she whispered. "Oh, look at that divan. The wood trim is exquisite. If you like that sort of thing, I mean."

I snorted. "I think everyone likes that sort of thing. It looks expensive," I said. "I have no clue what we're looking for, but let's look in the bedroom."

"I have a light on my phone. You take the bedroom and I'll check out the kitchen. I need a snack."

"Behave yourself," I warned and headed to the bedroom.

Celia's bedroom had a king-sized four-poster bed and was covered in a tacky hot pink and black leopard print bedspread. It wasn't what I imagined when she said her house was done in English antiques. Everything seemed to have fringed edges. Blue peacock feathers were arrayed on the wall near a large round mirror and there was a small gold lamp with a black and pink leopard print shade on the dresser. The whole place made me feel uncomfortable. Even if the owner wasn't dead, and we weren't sneaking around her house uninvited, it would have made me feel uncomfortable.

I sat on the edge of the bed and opened the bedside table's drawer. There was a pair of reading glasses, an old birthday card, two pens, and an address book. I slid the drawer closed.

The carpet was dark brown, thick, and plush. It reminded me of something out of the eighties. The closet door was covered in a mirror with a gold edged frame. I got up and opened the closet door, shining my flashlight on the contents. Celia had worn a lot of leopard print and I had always wondered if she had a closet full of leopard print clothes. Now I knew. She did.

I closed the closet door and opened the one next to it. The house was older and didn't have a walk-in closet, but there were these two long closets to accommodate the owner. I wondered why she didn't have a walk-in closet put in with all the clothes she owned. The other side of the closet was just as stuffed as the first. I flipped through the hangers but didn't see anything of interest.

As I was closing the door, I noticed a brown leather jacket hanging on the inside of the door. I pulled the door open wider and shined the light on the jacket. It was definitely a man's jacket, which wouldn't have been odd since Celia had a boyfriend, but it didn't look right. I took the hanger off the hook and held it up.

"Kitchen's clean. She buys caviar. Can you believe that? She was always so pretentious. What's that?" she asked, walking up behind me.

"Maybe she was celebrating something with the caviar," I said absently, looking the coat over. "It's a man's coat."

"So what's interesting about that? And what would she be celebrating?" she asked.

"How would I know? Maybe she and Gerald had something to celebrate," I said, looking through the coat pockets. They were empty. "Does this look like it would fit Gerald?"

"Maybe when he was in the sixth grade," she said peering at it.

"That's what I thought. I wonder who it belongs to?" I asked. The coat was much too small to fit Gerald. Maybe she had bought it for herself, not realizing it was a man's. I held it up to my nose and sniffed. I could faintly smell a man's cologne. It smelled familiar, but I couldn't quite place it.

"She only has the two daughters that I know of. No sons," Mom said. "Maybe Celia had someone on the side."

I nodded. "Weird. Or maybe she imported it from Britain and didn't realize it was a man's and not a woman's coat. That doesn't explain the cologne, though."

"Yeah, maybe," Mom said. "Anything else of interest in here?"

"Not really. The place is really clean and free of clutter. The closets are stuffed to the hilt, but everything seems neat and in order. I wonder if she has a storage shed somewhere. It seems like there should be more stuff," I said, looking around. My own bedroom was filled with things I had collected over the years.

Some might say it was a little cluttered. I didn't care. Super-neat freaks gave me the creeps.

"You're practically a hoarder. Other people don't live like that," Mom said, looking at the bed. "Celia sure had tacky taste. It's hard to believe when her flower arrangements were so pretty."

"Oh? You're going to admit she did nice work?" I asked hanging the coat up.

"Maybe. Now that she's dead, I have nothing to lose."

"That's big of you," I said and closed the closet door. "Let's take a quick look through the other rooms and then get out of here. I don't want to get caught."

We were done looking through the rest of the house in less than fifteen minutes, and sadly, there wasn't anything of any interest. I had hoped for something. Anything. If I could get the detective on someone else's trail, it would have given me peace of mind. We headed to the front door.

"Don't forget to wipe off that key," I said as Mom put the key under the mat.

"Oh," she said and wiped both sides against her shirt. "There." She held it by the edges and put it under the mat and stood up.

"Let's go," I said and we headed back to my car.

I hoped we hadn't left anything behind. Had I closed the bedroom door? I thought so, but now I couldn't remember. But something like that wouldn't have tipped off the detective, anyway. He had no idea if Celia kept her bedroom door open or closed.

"Let's get a chocolate shake," Mom said when we were in the car.

"I thought it was too many calories this late at night?"

She shrugged. "Calories schmalories."

I started the car and pulled away, heading in the direction of the closest McDonald's. We should have gone straight there and saved ourselves the trouble.

Chapter Fourteen

I'd tossed and turned all night long, thinking about what we'd found in Celia's house, which pretty much amounted to nothing other than a man's coat that was way too small for her boyfriend. Celia didn't have a son, and I had never heard of her having any nearby male relatives, although I hadn't spent a lot of time hanging out with her and getting to know her. The coat made my spidey senses tingle. Someone somewhere knew something about this murder. I just needed to figure out who that someone was.

Since I wasn't able to sleep, I got up and went to the kitchen to look through the cupboards for ideas for something to bake. That's what I did when I was stressed. I baked.

Chocolate is good for stress, so I baked up a batch of double chocolate chip muffins. The house smelled wonderful as they baked and by the time they were done, I was starving. I took a bite of one and the moist chocolately goodness was almost too much to bear. Someone would appreciate my efforts, and if I didn't get them out of the house, I was going to be sorry. They were impossible to ignore, and I didn't need the temptation. I packed them up into a basket, leaving one out for my mother.

I PUSHED OPEN THE DOOR to the British Coffee and Tea Company and my eyes immediately landed on Gerald Vance, sitting at a corner table brooding over a cup of coffee. I stopped in my tracks, willing him to look in my direction. When it didn't happen, I headed toward his table. I nodded at Agatha as I passed her.

"Hi Gerald, I brought you some muffins," I said, holding up the basket. Actually, I had brought them for Agatha in the hopes she would let me sell some of them in her shop. But never mind that now. It was a happy coincidence that Gerald was here and I decided to take advantage of it.

He stared at me as if trying to place me, grief clearly clouding his mind. When recognition showed on his face, he narrowed his eyes at me. "Why?"

"Well, I uh, I was just thinking about you. I know this is a difficult time for you and I thought I'd bring you some muffins," I said, suddenly feeling foolish. How do you say I brought muffins to make you feel better about the death of your girlfriend? My muffins were good, but they weren't that good.

He stared at the basket. "And you knew to look for me here?"

"I did," I said, hoping he wouldn't see the absurdity in that. If I could get him to talk, maybe he'd tell me something about Celia that would help with my investigation.

"Why?" he asked suspiciously.

I forced myself to smile. "I'm sorry for your loss, Gerald. I just didn't want you to feel alone in this. There are people who are concerned about you. We know you loved Celia."

He narrowed his eyes at me. "You and your mother didn't like Celia."

"What? No, that isn't true. Celia is hometown folk and we take care of our own here in Sparrow," I said, nodding. Celia might not have been my favorite person, but I wouldn't wish for anyone to be murdered.

He nodded slowly and looked at the basket again. "Okay."

"I'm so sorry for your loss," I repeated and pulled out a chair across from him. I hoped he didn't mind and when he didn't object, I set the basket between us on the table.

He nodded but didn't say anything.

"Here, help yourself," I said and scooted the basket toward him.

He reached into the basket, pushing back the dishtowel covering the muffins, and took one out. "Smells good."

"I hope you like them," I said glancing around the room. There were only four other people besides Agatha and her employee in the shop. That was good in case he got upset and didn't like me asking him questions.

He bit into the muffin and slowly smiled. "This is the best muffin I have ever tasted."

"Really? I'm glad you like it. I've worked on the recipe for what seems like ages. It's the sour cream that makes them so moist. Gerald, can you tell me who you think may have murdered Celia?"

He stopped chewing and looked at me. "I have no idea. I just know it was a horrible person. But I do think there's something odd about Sam. He seemed to like Celia a lot. And I mean a lot. It made me mad."

"What do you mean?" It was true that Sam bought oyster crackers especially for Celia, and he had stopped in the middle of a very busy lunch rush to appease her when she complained about me the day she died, but had he paid her undue attention? She was at least fifteen years older than Sam and she was emotionally high maintenance while Sam was laid back. I couldn't imagine that Sam had any interest in her.

"He sent her flowers," he said. "Who sends flowers to a florist?"

"Why did he do that?" I asked. "Where did he buy them?"

"Last year there was a waitress at the diner that was rude to the customers. She and Celia got into it and Sam sent her flowers to make up for it. From your mom's shop." He snorted. "Can you believe he bought the flowers from your mother's shop? It was a slap in the face if you ask me. And did he send flowers to all the customers that that waitress was rude to? Of course not! Celia said there was nothing to it, but I had to wonder. I loved her, you know."

I nodded trying to take all this in. Sam was nice, but I couldn't see him sending Celia flowers to make up for a rude waitress. But I could see Celia having trouble with a waitress, not to mention everyone else she met. That wouldn't surprise me at all.

"Maybe he was just being nice," I suggested.

He snorted. "Maybe he was and maybe he wasn't. I tell you, if I ever find out for sure that he killed Celia, I'd kill that little runt of a man."

I looked at him wide-eyed. "You don't want to be saying things like that, Gerald." I looked over my shoulder to see if anyone was eavesdropping, but no one seemed to be paying attention to us.

"Yeah, sure," he said. "All I know is my Celia is dead, and that pipsqueak was one of the last people to see her alive."

"Is there anything else that seemed off?" I asked. I didn't want to dwell on Sam with Gerald's open hostility toward him.

What he said seemed odd, and it made me wonder about Sam, but I had known him a long time. He couldn't hurt anyone.

He took another bite of the muffin and thought a moment. "Not that I can think of. Why are you asking me these questions?"

I shrugged. "I don't know. I just feel terrible about the whole thing. Like I said earlier, I know this must be hard for everyone involved."

He nodded and reached into his pocket, taking out three peppermints and laid them on the table. "Celia made me homemade peppermints. I have a whole bowl full, but they'll be gone soon. I'll miss them. They're good for indigestion."

I eyed them. They were individually wrapped in wax paper like saltwater taffy. "That's what my mother says."

"I've got things to do now. Thanks for the muffins."

I nodded, realizing I was being asked to leave and stood to my feet. "If I can do anything to help, don't hesitate to call," I offered.

"Sure."

"Do you mind if I take one of those peppermints? The coffee I drank earlier gave me coffee breath."

"Help yourself," he said dismissively.

"Thanks," I said and picked up one of the candies.

I headed over to Agatha at the far corner of the room. "Hi Agatha, I hope you don't mind me bringing muffins into the shop," I whispered as I sat at her table. "I was going to bring them to you, but I saw Gerald and I felt sorry for him. I promise to bring you some in the next day or two."

"Oh, that's fine," she said with a wave of her hand.

"Agatha, I was thinking that since I'm working on recipes for my new cookbook, maybe you could sell some baked goods here at the shop for me? What I'm really looking for is customer response, not necessarily making a profit from the sales."

"Oh, that sounds like an interesting idea. I'd love to sell some of your baked goods here. The customers would love them," she said, laying down her newspaper. "Did you get anything new from Gerald?" She whispered the last part, her eyes darting to where he sat.

I shook my head. "Not really. He doesn't seem to know anything." I decided not to mention that he had brought up Sam's name.

"I certainly hope they get this sorted out quickly," she said, stirring her tea.

"Me too," I said and unwrapped the peppermint.

Chapter Fifteen

"Hey Rainey, how are you?"

I looked up from my phone and smiled at John Callaway. We had gone to high school together what seemed like eons ago. "I'm great, John."

It had been ten days since Celia had died and John and I were standing in line at the British Tea and Coffee shop, waiting our turn. I had to be at work in less than an hour and I could have gotten coffee there, but the diner only served plain Jane coffee and I was in the mood for something a little fancier.

"Rainey, I've been meaning to ask if you'd like to go to a movie or something?" he asked with a hint of hope in his voice. John had blond hair and blue eyes and looked like an all-American high school football star. And that's exactly what he had been in school.

I looked up from my phone again. "Oh, you know, John, that's sweet of you. But, I'm still fresh off of a divorce and I don't think I'm ready. But if I were going to date, I'd love to go out with you." I'd run into John several times since I moved back to Sparrow and I knew the invitation was on the horizon. The unasked question always seemed eminent when we talked.

"Oh, okay, maybe another time then," he said sadly. Then he smiled. "I can understand that you need some time."

I nodded, feeling guilty even though there was nothing to feel guilty about. John was a good guy. I just wasn't ready to date. My cheating ex-husband had made me cautious.

I ordered a large mocha latte and found a seat at a corner table to read the latest book I had downloaded onto my phone.

"Rainey, how are you?" Agatha asked, pulling out a chair and sitting across from me.

I looked up from my phone and smiled. "I'm good. I'm heading to work in just a bit and I thought I'd stop by for some caffeine to put me in the mood."

There was a twinkle in her eyes when she smiled. "It's a lovely spring day, isn't it?"

"It certainly is," I agreed.

"Can an old woman stick her nose into your business?"

"Uh, sure," I said, wondering what she had in mind.

"Well, let me be straight with you. There's no use fiddle-faddling around when you've got something to say and since you said I could stick my nose in your business, I'll do just that. Rainey, you're a beautiful girl and you're still young. Don't waste away your days living in the past. Open your heart to at least try to love again."

I stared at her. This was the last thing I expected her to say. "I'm not living in the past. I'm just not ready yet."

To be honest, her words hurt a little. She was a sweet woman, and I knew she meant it kindly, but it stung. Was I wasting my days living in the past? The divorce was over. I had heard rumors that my ex-husband was dating, and it wasn't the woman he had cheated on me with. I didn't want him back, but I felt a twinge or two of jealousy whenever I thought about it.

She nodded. "I'm just saying, don't wait too long, darling. You can get used to being alone, and it gets hard to allow someone in."

"I won't," I said. "I'll keep your words in mind." I bit back the tears that threatened to fall and silently chided myself for them. I just wasn't ready yet. One day I would be, but not now.

CLAM CHOWDER AND A MURDER

She reached across the table and squeezed the back of my hand, then got up and left.

I inhaled deeply and then exhaled with a sigh. Was I living in the past? I didn't think so. But, maybe I was. It was something I would have to think about.

"I'VE GOT TO PICK UP my kids," Diane said. "Do you mind if I leave early, Sam?"

"Nah, go ahead," Sam said from where he stood cleaning the grill. The diner was closed, and we were finishing cleaning up and prepping for the next day.

I looked at Sam as he bent over the grill. Was Gerald right about Celia and Sam? I couldn't imagine the two of them together, but there was that smaller sized man's coat hanging in Celia's closet. A coat that looked as if it might fit Sam perfectly.

"What are you thinking about?" Sam asked, looking at me. He had stopped scrubbing the grill with the wire brush he held in his hand and was watching me.

"Oh. Nothing," I said, and went back to filling salt shakers.

He chuckled and went back to scrubbing the grill. "Looked like you were deep in thought for a minute there."

I looked at him again. "Sam, can I ask you something without you getting mad?"

He turned back to me. "Why would I get mad about something you asked?"

I shrugged. "Were you and Celia Markson seeing each other?" I said it fast, like that would make it easier.

His face fell. "Why would you ask that?"

I shrugged. "It seems like you bent over backward to make Celia happy when she came in. I don't know. It was a thought that I had. Plus, Gerald said he thought you were."

He was quiet for a moment. "What if I did? What would it matter? A person has a right to see whoever they want."

That was the last thing I expected to hear. I really thought he would deny it. "Really Sam? You were dating her? Why? There are plenty of women around here you could date. Women a lot closer to your age and not as obnoxious as Celia Markson. And didn't you feel weird that she was dating Gerald?"

"The real Celia wasn't the person you saw in here. When we were together, she was sweet and kind. I know it doesn't make sense to you, but there was just something about her."

"I'm shocked, Sam. I really am. Why did she keep Gerald around if she was with you? I can't see that Gerald is any more of a catch than Celia was. The two of them belonged together. I just can't imagine you being with her."

He tossed the wire brush down. "She and Gerald had broken up, so it's not like she wasn't free. And you're just judging her by what you saw. It was what you didn't see that made me want to be with her. But, she didn't want anyone to know she was with me." He said the last part with a hint of sadness in his voice and that surprised me as much as knowing he had dated her.

"Seriously? She didn't want people to know? You mean, she thought she was above you?" I asked. I couldn't imagine it. Sam as a great guy. He never raised his voice when we were late and he helped people in the community all the time. Everyone liked Sam.

CLAM CHOWDER AND A MURDER

He frowned. "I'm not educated. She thought I was beneath her. We argued about it and broke up a couple of weeks before she died. When she came in that day, I wanted to ask her to take me back, but I could tell from our conversation that she had lost all interest in me, so I didn't."

"Did you kill her?"

"What? No! I would never kill her or anyone else. How can you ask me that?" He stared at me incredulously.

I shrugged in embarrassment. "I knew you wouldn't. Do the police know you had been seeing her?"

He shook his head. "I'd rather not tell them."

"Why? What if they find out?" It didn't make sense to me. If Celia was the one that didn't want other people to know she was seeing him, what did it matter if people knew now that she was gone?

"Because I didn't tell the detective when he first questioned me. It will look bad if I tell him now."

"You're right, it will look bad if you tell him now. But why didn't you tell him when he first questioned us?" I felt like I was seeing a whole new side to Sam. One that didn't make sense to me in light of the Sam I had always known."

He shrugged and looked away. "Maybe I was glad no one knew that me and Celia were a thing. Maybe it bothered me a little that she was the one that broke up with me. I don't know why, but when he started questioning me, I just couldn't say it."

I sighed. "Sam, I think you need to talk to that detective before things get worse. What if he figures it out? What if Gerald tells him? What are you going to say when he shows up at your door asking you about it?"

"I don't know, Rainey. I just don't know," he said and turned back to the grill. "I didn't do it. I didn't kill Celia. I loved her. And Gerald never knew for sure that we were seeing each other. I'll just deny it if someone brings it up."

"You need to tell the detective the truth. Someone had to have seen you with her at some point in time. It would be terrible if the detective came back here and arrested you."

"We only went out in public when we went to Boise. No one saw us together."

I sighed. Sam was being obstinate. Or maybe just scared. "Do you have any idea who killed her?"

He shook his head and turned back toward me. "No. I can't imagine who it would be. But I will say that she wasn't feeling well for a while. She had sores on her tongue. Her mother died of mouth cancer when Celia was in her teens and she was worried she had it. I tried to get her to go to the doctor, but she wouldn't do it. She said she thought they would go away on their own. I think she was afraid to know for sure."

"I wonder if that had anything to do with how she died. You really need to tell the detective about the sores in her mouth. I'm sure they saw them during the autopsy, but they should know that she had them for some time. It might help them in some way."

"I told you, I can't tell him," he said and picked up the wire brush and turned back to the grill.

"Sam, this is going to look bad if the detective finds out you didn't tell him the truth," I said.

He didn't say anything more. I carried the salt shakers out to the tables. I knew Sam well enough to know he hadn't killed Celia. Didn't I?

Chapter Sixteen

CLAM CHOWDER AND A MURDER

I was filling in at my mom's flower shop the next day when Gerald came in. I looked up when the little bell over the door jingled. To say I was surprised to see him was an understatement.

"Hi Gerald," I said. I had been working on placing an order for supplies and trying to decide how many clear glass vases my mom might need. I don't know why she always waited until the last minute to place her supply order, but there was less than half a case of them left.

Gerald grunted and looked over at the refrigerated display case.

"What can I help you with?" I asked.

"I need something for Celia's funeral tomorrow."

I frowned. "Oh? You can look at the catalog for ideas on arrangements, or if you have something in mind, we can make it up for you." I wanted to ask him why he didn't have the arrangement made at Celia's shop, but I didn't want to seem rude.

He stepped up to the counter and opened one of the catalogs. "She liked yellow. What have you got in yellow?"

"We've got lots of yellow flowers. Sunflowers, daisies, roses or black-eyed Susans. I'm sure there are others in the back. Would you like me to take a look?"

He shook his head without looking up at me. "I'll find something in here." He pulled a peppermint out of his pocket and unwrapped it, then popped it into his mouth.

"I'm sorry about Celia," I said. I had said it before, but it seemed like I should say it again. "I'm sure half the town will turn out for her funeral. She'd have loved that." I'd heard that Celia had out of town relatives and the funeral had been pushed back a few days to accommodate them.

He looked up at me. "Are you? Are you really sorry?"

I stared at him for a minute, waiting for him to say something more. "Uh, yes. I am sorry. It's terrible," I said when he didn't continue.

He nodded, eyeing me. "It seems like you and your mother might be pleased she's gone."

I gasped. "Why would you say something like that, Gerald?"

He took a step forward and leaned down toward me. "Your mother doesn't have any competition now, does she? Celia said your mother's shop was struggling financially. Seems convenient she was killed, if you ask me."

I could smell the peppermint on his breath and it made me wonder. His demeanor was completely different from when I had brought him the muffins. He was more like he had been the day he came to the diner and accused Sam of killing Celia. "Gerald, I think that's a terrible thing to say. My mother's shop is not struggling financially and just because both Celia and my mother owned flower shops doesn't mean either my mother or myself are pleased she died. That's absurd."

"Is it? Is it really?" he asked, leaning forward. Gerald was so tall, that when he leaned toward me, it gave me pause. He may have been older, but I had the feeling he still had a lot of strength. I wondered if the peppermint was to mask the smell of alcohol because suddenly he seemed to be swaying just a bit.

"It is absolutely absurd. And why are you buying flowers for Celia here? Why aren't you buying them at her shop?" I didn't like his attitude, and I wished he would leave. There was no reason for him to buy flowers here.

CLAM CHOWDER AND A MURDER

"Because I wanted to come by and see if you and your mother were celebrating Celia's death." He stood up straight and glared at me. Now I noticed that his eyes were red, and he looked like he hadn't shaved in a few days.

"That's enough of that kind of talk," I warned. "I think you should take your business elsewhere. Neither my mother nor I am happy about Celia's death and I don't appreciate the accusation."

He snorted and glanced over his shoulder, then turned back to me. "I think we all know the truth here. You slipped Celia something in that clam chowder."

I shook my head and wished I wasn't in the shop alone with him.

"Listen, Gerald, I know this has been hard on you, but you're being ridiculous. I'm going to have to ask you to leave. I know Celia's flower shop has everything you need to have a nice arrangement made. Her assistants will make one up for you."

He placed both hands on the front counter and leaned toward me again. "Why don't you tell the truth? I told that detective it was you and your mother that killed my Celia. He agreed with me and said he was going to bring you both down to the police station and question you."

I slowly shook my head. "Please leave, Gerald. Now."

He stared at me, and then reached across the counter, grabbing me by the back of my head and pulling me toward him.

"No!" I screamed.

"I know what you did!"

I put both hands on his chest and pushed as he pulled me closer. The peppermint was cloyingly sweet as he exhaled his hot breath onto my face.

"Let me go!" I cried.

His grip tightened on the back of my head and I pushed harder against his chest. I was in good shape, and still took kickboxing classes, but the counter between us made it nearly impossible to get a punch in.

"Tell the truth!" he shouted.

"Let me go!" I said and hit him from beneath, landing a punch to his throat.

He made a croaking sound and let me go, taking a step back and putting his hands to his throat. I took the opportunity to grab my cell phone from beneath the counter and hit 911. I laid the phone down on the counter to keep both of my hands free.

"Hey!" he choked out and stumbled around the side of the counter to where I was.

"I need help at 4015 Raspberry Lane," I shouted toward the cell phone as he reached for me again. I punched him in the chest and pulled my arm back to get another one in.

He swore under his breath and blocked the next punch with his forearm. "I know what you did and I am not going to jail for it."

"Go to jail for what?" I asked and kicked him in the thigh. "I need police at 4015 Raspberry Lane," I repeated loudly in case the 911 operator hadn't been on the line the first time I said it.

He crumpled and slumped over in pain and groaned. "I'll get you," he seethed.

Then I remembered the peppermints. Celia had asked for one when she came into the diner because she said she had run out of them. It seemed Gerald was never without one and he was standing next to Celia's table while she ate her clam chowder.

"You did it, didn't you?" I asked, realizing the truth. "You killed Celia, but you're trying to get me to take the blame."

He looked up from his place on the floor and grinned. "She had it coming. That detective believes you did it. I thought he'd have arrested you before now. That's really what I came here to check out. But here you are, standing free as you please." He grunted and rocked himself onto his knees.

I kicked him in the face before he could get to his feet. "You evil man," I said and kicked him again, this time in the chest.

He groaned, cursing me, and fell to the floor.

"You'll pay for killing Celia," I said, picking up my cell phone and climbing the front counter to keep from having to pass him to get out of the shop. The 911 operator was trying to get me to talk to her. "I need an officer here at Sparrow Florist. Now."

I made it over the front counter and crossed the shop to the front door, breathing hard. Sirens sounded in the distance and I pushed the front door open. Gerald didn't appear to be following me, but I kept walking in case he got his second wind. I was not going to be his next victim.

Chapter Seventeen

CLAM CHOWDER AND A MURDER

I looked up as the diner door swung open. It was the lull between breakfast and lunch and the only people in the diner were an elderly couple in the far corner nursing a pot of coffee and reading the morning paper.

He pinned me with his dark green eyes and gave me a genuine smile. It was a first for the detective.

"How are you this morning?" I asked him, tossing the white dishtowel I had just used to dry my hands on over my shoulder.

"I'm fine now that we have our killer behind bars. How are you doing?" he asked and sat on one of the stools at the front counter.

"I'm a little stiff in my shoulder from throat punching that lousy killer," I said. "Can I get you something?"

"Coffee would be great."

I turned and filled a cup with plain Jane coffee from the carafe on the counter behind me. One of these days I was going to get Sam to sell fancier coffee. For now, it was old reliable. "Blueberry tart? On the house. I've been working on the recipe."

"Sounds great," he said with a nod of his head.

I set the coffee down in front of him and cut a piece of the tart. "So, did he confess?"

He nodded again. "He did. Seems he thought Celia was cheating on him. With Sam. It's funny, Sam didn't mention he was seeing Celia when I interviewed him."

I lifted an eyebrow and set the tart down in front of him. "Sam said Celia had broken up with Gerald. I suppose she was free to see whoever she wanted." I didn't want to comment on why Sam hadn't told him about his relationship with Celia.

"I think Gerald hoped either Sam or you would be blamed for poisoning Celia with tainted clam chowder. He thought Sam might have wanted to get back at her for dumping him. But when I told him we didn't have a sample of the chowder, he redirected me to look at you and your mother. He said your mother viewed Celia as stiff competition and she would stop at nothing to eliminate her. You, of course, being her daughter, had to have helped by poisoning her clam chowder."

I rolled my eyes. "Right. Because the florist profession is so cut-throat competitive, one has to eliminate the competition. Literally."

He chuckled. "He was convinced they were getting married, even though Celia told him a month ago that she was done. Her daughter told us her mother had broken it off with him."

"Really?" I asked. "I guess you can convince yourself of anything if you want it to be true desperately enough."

"I guess you can. When Celia wouldn't change her mind, he killed her and then put the ad in the paper to reinforce the picture of him being a grieving boyfriend. He kept insisting it was you and your mother that killed her, but I just had a feeling about the two of you. I didn't think either of you could be killers," he said and took a sip of his coffee.

"Oh, you just knew we couldn't be killers? But you made us feel like you suspected us?" I asked, putting my hands on my hips. This guy was something else.

He grinned. "It's not wise to show all your cards. Something may be gained by keeping them close to the vest."

I narrowed my eyes at him. "Thanks a lot."

"But, regardless of Gerald's reasons for murder, you can't kill someone for breaking up with you. At least, not in Idaho you can't."

"How did he do it?" I asked, leaning on the front counter now. "He slipped something into her clam chowder that day she died? Right? I saw him at her table that day. It was really busy in here and I never got a chance to check on her after I served her the clam chowder." The sun shining through the window made me squint.

He nodded. "Arsenic. He had been slipping small amounts of it to her for a while. Apparently, he made some homemade peppermint candies and coated them with it. Peppermint is a nice strong flavor that will disguise some flavors. He slipped it into her tea as well, hoping it would build up in her body and eventually kill her. He didn't admit to putting it in the clam chowder, but I'd say it's a good guess that he did."

I shook my head. "He told me Celia made the peppermints. How terrible for Celia. I didn't like her much, but she didn't deserve to die like that."

"Indeed. No one does." He picked up his fork and took a bite of the tart. "Wow, this is really good. Do you bake a lot?"

I smiled, biting back a sarcastic answer. How could he know I was a professional cook and baker? That was a lifetime ago.

"I do a bit of baking and cooking now and then."

He nodded. "You should do it professionally. This is really good."

"I'll consider it," I said and took the dishtowel off my shoulder and wiped down the front counter.

"I'm sorry I led you to believe you and your mother were under suspicion."

I glanced at him. "No problem. You were just doing your job."

He nodded. "I was. I hope neither of you will take it personally. I'm moving to Sparrow and I would hate to have made enemies this quickly."

"Nope. We Dayes' don't take that sort of thing personally."

He snorted and took a sip of his coffee. "I bet you don't."

I shook my head and suppressed a mile. The detective was a smart aleck. I like smart alecks.

Author Notes

I hope you enjoyed reading about Rainey, her mother, and her sister Stormy as much as I enjoyed writing about them. They're a little smart alecky, but they have a very close family dynamic. I think I enjoy writing characters that are a little silly and maybe even a little irreverent the best. You never know what they might say or do!

Follow me on Facebook: www.facebook.com/759206390932120[1]

And Bookbub: https://www.bookbub.com/authors/kathleen-suzette

---

1. http://www.facebook.com/759206390932120

Made in the USA
Lexington, KY
30 June 2019